UNDER THE EYE OF GOD
AN ISAAC SIDEL NOVEL

UNDER THE EYE OF GOD
AN ISAAC SIDEL NOVEL

JEROME CHARYN

MYSTERIOUSPRESS.COM

3 1336 09132 2041

OPEN ROAD

INTEGRATED MEDIA
NEW YORK

Cover design by Mumtaz Mustafa

ISBN 978-1-4532-7099-8

Published in 2012 by MysteriousPress.com/Open Road Integrated Media
180 Varick Street
New York, NY 10014
www.mysteriouspress.com
www.openroadmedia.com

Hereby it is manifest, that during the time men live without a common power to keep them in awe, they are in that condition which is called war; and such a war, as is of every man, against every man . . . the same is consequent to the time, wherein men live without other security, than what their own strength, and their own invention shall furnish them withal. In such condition, there is no place for industry; because the fruit thereof is uncertain; and consequently no culture of the earth; no navigation, no use of commodities that may be imported by the sea . . . no knowledge of the face of the earth; no account of time; no arts; no letters; no society; and which is worst of all, continual fear, and danger of violent death; and the life of man, solitary, poor, nasty, brutish, and short.

—Thomas Hobbes, *Leviathan*, 1651

PART ONE

1

VICTORIES MEANT LITTLE TO ISAAC SIDEL. He despised election campaigns, with their pomp and panoply, their bitter battles. He went up to the Bronx without his Secret Service man. He loved to stand on some hill and look down upon the firebombed streets. All that desolation seemed to soothe him. The Big Guy needed a strong pinch of chaos. That meadowland of gutted buildings had a strange beauty, like a diorama of brick teeth.

He stood alone in Claremont Park and what he saw pricked his curiosity. Land surveyors and army engineers had climbed onto another hill with their tripods and magical measuring devices. This was no citizen's group. An MP was guarding their equipment.

The Big Guy hiked over to the army engineers. They saluted him.

"Hello, Mr. President."

"Jesus," Isaac said, "I'm not in line to become your commander in chief. You're looking at the bottom half of the ticket."

The chief engineer smiled at him. There was no menace in his manner, no hidden darting of his eyes.

"You're still our president," he said.

"But what are you guys doing here? The Bronx isn't much of a playground."

"This is a practice session, sir. My engineers have to get used to all terrain."

He produced a permit, signed by the NYPD. It still bothered Isaac—the cavalry invading Claremont Park. But he wouldn't badger these engineers. They continued with their work.

"Good-bye, Mayor Sidel."

He couldn't disappear without creating a little storm of autograph seekers. He signed "Sidel" on bits of cardboard and the bills of baseball caps. A woman caressed his sleeve.

"We don't want Michael," she whispered. "We want you."

Isaac skulked out of the park while the army engineers surveyed the South Bronx from their hill. His fans saluted him from fire escapes across the street. There was little Isaac could do about all the fury surrounding the election.

It was known as the slaughter of '88. Democrats battered Republicans, knocked them out of the box. President Calder Cottonwood couldn't even capture his own state. He lost Arizona in the very same landslide. But the Democratic Party was riddled with rancor. Its standard bearer, J. Michael Storm, the czar of baseball and president-elect, was sinking fast in the polls. He was a flagrant Casanova. One of his mistresses had surfaced since the election and demanded hush money from the Dems. The Party would have to pay and pay and pay.

That wasn't the worst of it. The Dems had to cover up J. Michael's crooked land deals, the phony corporations he'd started with Clarice, his dipsomaniac of a wife. It's lucky he had a running mate like Sidel, a former police commissioner who ran around with a Glock in his pants and captured criminals while he was on the campaign trail.

The Party couldn't have won the election without Sidel. He was much more popular than a president or a baseball czar. He should have resigned his mayor's job, but the citizens of New York wanted Isaac to govern them until the day he ran off to DC. Michael had moved into the Waldorf with his transition team. But Isaac stole whatever little thunder J. Michael had left with his daily shenanigans. And so the Dems had to get him out of Manhattan.

Tim Seligman, the Party's chief strategist, who'd been a fighter pilot in Nam, decided to send Isaac out on the road on some kind of quixotic quest. He could scream his head off about any subject under the sun as long as he didn't mention J. Michael Storm. He was given his own touring bus, a gift from the Democratic National Committee. And Tim Seligman accompanied him as his babysitter. They flew to Dallas, where Isaac began his tour of Texas. He was the Democrats' holy warrior. But he couldn't ride with Marianna Storm, Michael's twelve-year-old daughter, who was known as the Little First Lady. Voters had fallen in love with her during the election. She didn't campaign with her father. She was always at Isaac's side. The Big Guy needed a "consort." Marianna had camped out with him at Gracie Mansion, because she couldn't bear her mother and father, and had baked butternut cookies for Isaac and his staff. Now, Seligman banned her from Isaac's bus, and Isaac turned on Tim, threatened to resign as the Democrats' holy warrior unless he had the Little First Lady. But Tim had to deal with all the postelection flak. The Dems had a photo of Calder pissing in the Rose Garden and threatened to release it if the Republican machine continued to harp on Michael's mistresses.

"Isaac, it's a war out there," Tim said. "The bombs are flying. Do you want to ruin that little girl?"

"By having her sit with me?"

"The Republicans are concocting a very tall tale. And how can we fight it? Unless Marianna disappears, they'll accuse you of having a Lolita complex."

"What Lolita?"

"Isaac, it's a smear. They're talking pedophilia."

The future vice president jumped on Tim, rocked the entire bus. The Secret Service had to separate them. The boss of Isaac's detail, Martin Boyle, an Oklahoman who was six foot two, had to beg the Big Guy.

"Sir, if I let you go, will you promise to behave?"

"Not before I murder Tim."

"Then I'll hold you here until kingdom come."

"Perfect. I won't have to tour Texas."

"And President Cottonwood will jump on our backs," Tim said. "He's behind the smear. We went deep into Calder's pockets. We captured his astrologer."

"Calder has an astrologer? He's like fucking Adolf Hitler."

"He can't make a move without her. He's beside himself."

"What's her name?" Isaac had to ask.

"Markham, Mrs. Amanda Markham."

"And how did you capture her, huh, Timmy? The Prez must have guarded this Amanda with his life."

"She walked."

"Of her own free will? That's a peach. She comes into our camp and offers her services, and you don't smell a rat? What's the matter with you? Calder's crazed, so he lends us his favorite spy."

"Isaac, we're not dummies. We checked her out. We have tapes of her with the Prez."

The Big Guy wasn't amused. "You've been bugging the White House? Boyle, did you hear that?"

"No," said Isaac's Secret Service man. "I'm not allowed to listen to your conversations, sir. I'm only here to protect your life."

"I can't believe it. Nothing makes sense. . . . And what did you learn from the tapes, Timmy Boy?"

"A lot. About Calder's pedophilia play. He's been doctoring photographs. Of you and Marianna. And that's when Mrs. Markham started to rebel."

"Why?"

"It disgusted her. She's a big fan of yours. The Prez found out, and he broke her nose. That's when she walked."

"Where is this Mata Hari?"

"On the bus, and she's not Mata Hari."

"She climbed aboard, and you never told me?"

"I wanted Amanda to study you without your being aware of her. She's an astrologer, the best in the business. She's preparing your chart. She can help us plot our future . . . yours and the Party's."

"Damn you," Isaac said. "You steal Marianna and saddle me with a fucking star clerk."

"Who's a star clerk?"

Isaac had to crane his neck, or he couldn't have discovered the source of that shrill cry. A roly-poly woman was perched at the back of the bus with a bandage on her nose. She hadn't entered his field of vision until now. He should have noticed her. He'd been the Commish.

"Sidel, do you have a sore throat?"

He blinked at the fat witch. "How did you guess?"

"Taureans have a lot of problems with their throats. . . . "

"Does Calder have the same affliction?"

"I never discuss my other clients," she said.

"But you did talk to Tim about Marianna, and he took her from me."

"That's different. The child was in danger, and so were you. Sidel, I'm your survival kit."

"I doubt that. You were Calder's clairvoyant . . . until he broke your nose."

"But I couldn't save him. Nobody can."

"Why? Was the moon in Virgo the moment he was born? And it captured his capriciousness?"

"You're making fun of me, Sidel."

"Yes, ma'am. Marianna's the only moon I'll ever need."

■ ■ ■

HE'D CREATED MERLIN ON ACCOUNT of Marianna. She couldn't function near her mom and dad, with all their feuds. She sulked like a diva, and Isaac had to do something. He brought her up to the badlands of the Bronx. They boycotted Robert Moses' Cross Bronx

Express, which had ruined neighborhood after neighborhood, ripping into the Bronx's fabric, destroying it a patch at a time. Isaac couldn't save the borough, but he could rescue some of its kids. So he started Merlin, a school away from school, where the brainiest kids of a firebombed Bronx could meet with the best little wizards of Manhattan right inside the mayor's mansion. And Isaac had recruited Marianna—to enrich his own life, along with the wayward boys and girls of the Bronx. She began spending more time with him at Gracie Mansion. She ironed the Big Guy's shirts, took over the kitchen, and baked butternut cookies. He couldn't have survived without her. He also pitied Marianna, who had such a dismal mom and dad.

Now he was with that witch, Mrs. Markham, in the middle of Texas. He had his Glock and his own sixth sense. But he couldn't understand why Timmy was with him in a yellow campaign bus and hadn't returned to J. Michael, who stumbled wherever he went.

"Michael needs you, Tim."

"He's beyond repair," the strategist said. "My one consolation is that Calder sank faster than he did. It's a first in American politics. A presidential race where both guys couldn't light the simplest fucking fire. If you get stuck in some scandal, Michael will disappear *with* the Waldorf. That's why I couldn't let Calder lock you into a Lolita complex. I had to grab Marianna."

They'd arrived in San Antone, where Tim had scheduled a press conference in the old cattlemen's bar at the Menger Hotel, across from the Alamo. The Dems wanted to turn Isaac into Davy Crockett, tear off his Manhattan skin. But Isaac wouldn't fiddle with his own temperament, play some lost son of San Antonio. He wouldn't wear cowboy boots, like other politicians, attend horse shows, or spit into a solid-gold spittoon. He talked about the blight of inner city schools in the '80s, the eleven-year-old pistoleros who worked for drug lords and shot rival gangs to pieces, because they couldn't be tried in open court.

"I don't like coca kings hiding behind the skirts of children."

"Then what do you like?" one of the reporters asked. "This is Crockett country. Would you hamper us with a gun-control bill?"

"I might," Isaac said, "if I could get rid of eleven-year-old assassins."

"This isn't Brooklyn. Our kids don't play with guns. We'd slap them silly, sir."

The fat witch bumped into Isaac. "Make it short," she whispered.

"Christ, Mrs. Markham. Are you my chief of staff?"

"The moon is in the middle of two houses. That's dangerous. You're on the cusp of something I don't like at all. Scatter as fast as you can."

"Run away from the Alamo? This is Texas, dear."

"Don't patronize me," Mrs. Markham hissed and dug an elbow into Isaac's back . . . as some crazy shooter appeared in the crowd. This shooter had caught Martin Boyle and his Secret Service men with their pants down. They'd been foraging through the Menger Bar for possible kooks and had landed on their own blind side. The shooter had been difficult to spot. He was dressed as a military man, with a silver eagle on his shoulder. But he had a thick, heavy tongue and eyes shot with blood. His mouth sat crooked on his face, as if someone had sewn it there.

"I'm the eye of god," the shooter shouted, clutching a silver Colt with the longest barrel Isaac had ever seen. The Big Guy couldn't grab his own Glock. He would have brought pandemonium to the Menger, might have started a massacre. He shielded Mrs. Markham and a little girl, who'd come to seek his autograph, thrust them out of the line of fire, and leapt on the shooter, who squeezed his trigger once, clipped Isaac, grazed him under the arm. The chandeliers rang like celestial chimes. But why, why did Isaac think of those army engineers on their hill in the Bronx just as he was about to topple? It had to be a sinister sign.

"The Citizen's down, the Citizen's down," the Secret Service men sang into their button mikes. "The Citizen" was Isaac's code name inside the Service. They'd already captured the shooter; four of them, including Boyle, were lying on top of Isaac. Boyle's own cheeks were covered in Isaac's blood.

"Boyle," Isaac whispered, "will you get the fuck off? I can't breathe."

And then he blacked out.

2

H E WOKE IN A HOSPITAL room at Brooke Army Medical Center that must have been reserved for generals. It was bigger than Isaac's bedroom at Gracie Mansion. He had tubes connected to his arm and a plug in his nose that fed him oxygen. This hospital was part of Fort Sam Houston. Isaac had read about Fort Sam when he was still a boy. It was where Geronimo and his own Apache generals had once been held as prisoners of war. . . .

He shut his eyes, and when he woke again, he no longer had the tubes or the plug in his nose. Doctors and nurses had come and gone. They all wore military uniforms. Boyle was near his bed.

"It shouldn't have happened, Mr. President."

"Boyle, do I have to tell you again? I'm nobody's president. I'll be Michael's VP, if I live that long."

"Yes, Mr. President. But it shouldn't have happened. We were sloppy. It's unforgivable."

"What about the shooter? Is he hurt?"

"No, sir. He's fine. He's back in the hospital, under restraint."

9

"Did you see the fucking size of his Colt? Where did he get a gun like that?"

"It's a stage prop, sir. He swiped it from a rodeo."

"What's his name, Boyle?

"Billy Bob Archer. He's a Korean War vet."

"Korea? He looks like a baby. I'd have sworn he was even too young for Nam."

"It's the tunic, sir. It disguised his age. He's touching sixty, and he has a whole sheet of mental problems."

"Will they charge him with anything, Boyle?"

"Probably, sir. But I can't get involved with local law enforcement."

Tim Seligman came into the room with an enormous folder of press clippings.

"You're a hero, goddamn. The whole planet's raving about you, Isaac. You should see what they wrote in China and Pakistan. *Vice president-elect risks his life to safeguard an entire hotel from mad gunman.*"

"Where's Mrs. Markham?"

"Hiding somewhere. We had to block her out of the story. People might get the idea that you have your own personal astrologer. It's bad for politics."

"But she is my astrologer. And she saved my ass. I'd never have noticed the shooter if it hadn't been for . . . "

The telephone rang.

"Is that J. Michael? Did you tell him to call me, Tim?"

Isaac picked up the phone and growled into the receiver. "Sidel here."

It was the White House switchboard. Calder Cottonwood was on the line.

"How are you, son?"

"I feel like I'm living in a palace."

"I reserved that room for you. It's the best in the house. I'm still commander in chief, you know. And military hospitals are under my domain. . . . Is Tim Seligman there?"

"Yes, Mr. President."

"That scumbag, he's holding Markham a prisoner . . . in one of the Menger's back rooms."

"It's politics. Tim's playing hardball, like you."

There was a moment of silence. "Hardball?"

"Didn't you break her nose?"

"That was passion, not politics."

"Well, I'm just as passionate about Marianna Storm. And I hate losing her, Mr. President, just because your lads have decided to call me a cop with a Lolita complex, a fucking pedophiliac. Do I have your promise that your little game will end?"

"I could promise you the sun and moon, Sidel, but my boys and girls will clobber you if they can."

Isaac hung up on Calder Cottonwood. "Tim, I'd like to consult with my astrologer, please."

"That's impossible."

"Shall I fetch her myself? I'll knock on every fucking door at the Menger. I'll go there in my hospital gown."

Tim whispered into his button mike, and Mrs. Markham appeared. He must have taken her out of storage at the Menger and kept her in Isaac's yellow bus. She was very pale. She'd probably realized that the Dems were as capricious as Calder.

"Mrs. Markham, where would you put the eye of God? I mean, in what part of the Zodiac, what particular house?"

"I'm not equipped to answer that question."

"But that's what the mad soldier said. 'I'm the eye of God.' And you saw him coming, you anticipated him."

She stared at the wall. "I'm not equipped to answer that question."

"Timmy, what have you done to her? There are worse things than breaking a woman's nose. . . . Boyle, will you find my pants? I'm taking a stroll."

"You can't leave," Tim said. "There are a hundred reporters outside this room. You aren't ready to face them."

"Boyle, do you have my Glock?"

"Yes, Mr. President."

"Good. Then dress me, please."

Isaac sat up in bed, and Boyle shucked off his hospital gown. Isaac's ribs were taped. Boyle helped him into his shirt, pants, and shoes. Isaac wore a corduroy jacket that he'd picked up at a bargain counter in Waco. He looked like a catcher of criminals, a philosopher-clown.

"What's our destination?" Boyle asked.

"Billy Bob Archer."

Timmy groaned. "Isaac, they won't let us into the lunatics' ward."

"Wanna bet?"

"You're not to walk with Amanda Markham. We have to camouflage her as a volunteer."

"Come on. She's been on Letterman and Larry King. She's a star clerk. The biggest in the business. Didn't you say that?"

"She just happened to be near you when the gunman got there, thanks to Boyle's negligence."

"Don't knock Boyle. He can't attend to all the crazies."

"He should have been guarding you. That's what he's paid for."

"Tim, don't irritate me."

And Isaac sailed out of the room, holding Mrs. Markham's hand.

"The Citizen's up and running," Boyle sang into his mike, and the Secret Service had to clear a path for Isaac and prevent reporters from crushing him.

"Mr. Sidel, do you believe in the stars?"

"Ah, the real question is: Do the stars believe in me?"

"But don't you and the president share the same astrologer?"

"Ladies and gentlemen, Mrs. Markham is just a friend."

"Who's your biggest hero, Sidel?"

"AR," Isaac said without a bit of hesitation.

"AR? Did he die at the Alamo?"

"Nah. He was a gambler, the king of crime. Arnold Rothstein."

"Rothstein," Seligman hissed into Isaac's ear. "You'll sink us, for Christ's sake."

And Boyle steered the whole menagerie down one flight to the mental ward, where Isaac was stopped by an army captain and two MPs.

"Sorry, sir," the captain said, "but you can't go in there. It's off-limits, even to vice presidents."

"Do you have a phone, Captain?"

Isaac rang the White House, screamed until the switchboard put him through to President Cottonwood.

"Isaac, I'm on the crapper. What the hell do you want? I thought we'd finished talking."

"I found Mrs. Markham. You owe me one. I'd like to get into the mental ward and see Billy Bob, but the captain says no."

"Who's Billy Bob?"

"The man who tried to shoot up the Menger."

"But he's a nutcase. I can't interfere."

"Aren't you commander in chief?"

Isaac handed the telephone to the captain, who listened, mumbled a few words, put down the phone, and saluted Isaac.

"Captain," Isaac said, "Mrs. Markham goes with me."

"But the president said . . . "

"Do I have to call the White House again? It's absolutely critical that Mrs. Markham meet with Billy Bob."

The captain unlocked the gate to the mental ward.

Seligman seemed chagrined. "Isaac, shouldn't I—"

"No," Isaac said, and swept Mrs. Markham through the gate without Tim or Martin Boyle. They'd entered a kind of no-man's-land, a long, long corridor, with an MP marching in front of them.

"Isaac, I'm touched," said the astrologer, "that you took me into the cave with you."

"Shut up," Isaac said. He grabbed Mrs. Markham and pulled the bandage off her nose. She didn't scream. Nothing was broken or bruised.

"You're an actress, aren't you, playing Mrs. Markham?"

The roly-poly woman nodded her head.

"Poor Tim. Thinks he's bugging the White House. Calder has the best National Security boys. He lets Tim record whatever traffic he wants Tim to hear. What's your name?"

"Amanda . . . Amanda Wilde."

"You come into our camp with your little bona fides, and you're paid to unravel me. Isn't that right, Mrs. Wilde?"

"Yes . . . but I'm not married. I'm only—"

"Where did you pick up your astrology?"

"From a book."

"But you warned me at the Menger Bar . . . about Billy Bob."

"An actress's intuition. I felt—"

"Wait a minute. Is Billy Bob Archer an actor, too? Does he come from your own little company? Or is he one of Calder's commandos?"

"I don't . . . he shot you, didn't he?"

"A trifle. Calder could have risked a little flesh wound . . . if he had a marksman on his hands."

"At the Menger? Where people could . . . "

The MP brought them into a tiny cell that was isolated from the rest of the ward. Billy Bob Archer wasn't lying in bed. He sat in a leather chair, with his arms and legs shackled, and Isaac wondered if he was caught in the middle of some crazy drama.

"Billy Bob, remember me?"

"Yeah."

"Why would God lend His eye to you?"

"He didn't lend. I'm God's only eye."

"Then the Lord Himself is blind."

"That's right, Mr. Fancy Pants. And I've got to lead Him out of the darkness. Who's the fat girl?"

"My astrologer."

The shooter smiled. "Then she knows that you were born in God's house."

"Is that why you came after me with a cannon, Billy Bob? What's my birthday got to do with God?"

"A May baby is a mournful baby. . . . She knows."

Isaac inched up to the leather chair. "What does she know? Does God live at the White House? Does He have dreams in the Oval Office? Did Calder Cottonwood hire you?"

The shooter started to cry. "You're desecrating me. I had a mission. To shoot your eyes out. And I failed . . . on account of the fat girl."

"What the hell is going on?"

The ward's chief resident arrived in Billy Bob's cell. He was furious with Isaac, this army psychiatrist who was also a colonel. Trevor Welles. He had the whitest hair Isaac had ever seen on a man.

"This is a psychiatric ward, Mr. Mayor. It doesn't welcome nonsense."

"Aw, Doc," the shooter said. "Don't pick on the May baby."

"Do I have to gag you again, Corporal Archer?"

"But I want to hear what the fat girl has to say. Did you see God at the Menger, missy?"

Amanda blinked. "I'm not sure," she said. "I'm not sure."

Isaac kept looking at Welles' uniform: it seemed a little too familiar. "Colonel, did Billy Bob steal your tunic and wear it at the Menger?"

"Yes."

"How did he get his hands on it?"

"Is this an interrogation? You shouldn't even be here. . . . He broke into my locker."

"And got past two MPs at the big gate?"

"This is a hospital, not a prison."

"Did you coach him, Colonel Welles? Did you scrub him proper, lend him a rodeo gun?"

"Sir," the colonel said, "you will have to vacate this ward immediately."

"Not until I say good-bye to Billy Bob."

Isaac bent over the leather chair, kissed the shooter on the forehead. "My poor sweet Bob."

Then he clutched Amanda's hand, marched past Colonel Welles and his white, white hair, and got to the gate. His shadow, Martin Boyle, was on the other side of the thick, brutal wire. His hands were twitching. "You shouldn't have gone in there all alone."

"Alone?" Isaac said. "I had Amanda to protect me."

There was still a mob of reporters near the gate.

"Mr. Sidel, Mr. Sidel, did you meet with the crazy assassin?"

"Billy Bob's not an assassin. He mistook me for someone else."

"Who, sir?"

"A heavenly angel," Isaac said, and turned to his shadow.

"Call our driver, Boyle. Tell him to rev up the bus. We're getting out of San Antone."

■ ■ ■

THE BUS APPEARED OUTSIDE THE medical center in nine minutes. Isaac hopped aboard with the reporters who were covering his romp through Texas. He had a secretary and a small staff, but he almost never used them. He had no deals to cut. He wasn't a political strategist, like Tim. He was a hooligan with a gun. He got into fistfights. He had scars all over his body, like God's own warrior. He watched Amanda, waited until she sat down. He didn't want to panic his astrologer. And he didn't have to signal to Tim.

Seligman approached Isaac, sat down.

"We have to dump the bitch. . . . Isaac, she's in the public eye. My people checked. She's a plant."

"Timmy, darling, did they also check that your wire at the White House is a piece of fiction? Calder has his own script. He sucked you in."

"That's a lie."

16

Isaac stroked Tim's ear. "The ruckus at the Menger was a little assassination party. Amanda must have balked at the last minute. . . . Use your bean, Tim. How did Billy Bob waltz out of a locked facility in a colonel's uniform . . . and who supplied the cannon?"

"If it was Calder, I'll kill him. And I'll grab the bitch, make a citizen's arrest."

"You'll do nothing, Tim. We can't prove a thing. Calder will laugh at us. Then he'll grind me into the dirt. We'll look like amateurs, hurling assassination theories at the president of the United States. . . . What's our next stop?"

"Houston," Tim said.

"Good. Wake me when we get there."

And the Citizen fell fast asleep.

3

SAAC TOURED THE HOUSTON SHIP Channel, rode the mechanical bull at Gilley's, kneeled inside the Rothko Chapel, where he found a bit of peace contemplating that eccentric millionaire, Mark Rothko, who couldn't afford to buy an overcoat and would freeze his ass every winter . . . until he finally killed himself. Rothko's paintings, with their stark ribbons of color, soothed the Citizen, forced him to recognize his own isolation, the symbolic overcoat that he, too, would never wear.

He dialed his mavens at City Hall. He couldn't get that team of army engineers in Claremont Park out of his mind. His mavens did some digging on their own. The engineers were still around. Claremont Park had become their headquarters. They'd gone across the ruined meadowland of Morrisania with their magic tripods, surveying all the rubble and burnt bricks. Morrisania was a beggar's paradise. It suffered from more poverty than any other district in the whole United States. Isaac didn't like conundrums. He called the Pentagon, got some unctuous colonel on the line.

"Army engineers in the Bronx, Mr. Sidel? It must be a training mission."

"Training for what?"

The colonel couldn't say. There was a long silence until another colonel crept onto the wire.

"They have no authorization, Mr. Sidel. They shouldn't have gone into your backyard. And I'm sorry about the shooting in San Antone. The president has stuck a stick up our ass for allowing it to happen. We all hope you've recovered."

His mavens at City Hall got back to him in a couple of hours. The army engineers had disappeared from Claremont Park. But the Big Guy wasn't satisfied. Something still galled him, and he wasn't even sure what it was.

He returned to New York without Amanda, tried to ring up Marianna Storm, but couldn't seem to get her on the line. The Democrats had locked her out of his life. *Lolita.* And Isaac did what he often did when he was very blue. He camped outside the Ansonia, like some lost soul. It was his personal pilgrimage, deep as history. The Ansonia *was* history to Isaac Sidel. David Pearl had lived there, Arnold Rothstein's last pupil. Ah, if only he'd been born a bit earlier, and had met Rothstein on the Ansonia's stairs. AR might have taught Isaac a trick or two. . . .

He made his first pilgrimage to the Ansonia around 1940. It was a castle that rose above Broadway like some Alhambra with curving balconies and turreted rooftops, where kings could rule and play with or without their mistresses and wives. This castle was a whole block long. Isaac's dad, Joel Sidel, a glove manufacturer, would visit his silent partner, David Pearl, who had his own turret. Pearl was a boy wonder, twenty-five or so, and already a recluse.

Isaac would accompany his dad, sit in that turret, while Joel talked to David and drank champagne that had a slightly bluish color. There was a fever about the war in Europe, and the boy banker had helped Joel secure a contract from the army for "foul-weather gloves." The contract should have gone to a manufacturer with much deeper pockets, but it was David who understood the dynamics of a bidding war, and the particular palms he had to "smear." Joel was like a baby in the land of politics, but he could produce the finest kidskin gloves. David himself had a hundred pairs.

He was a smallish, almost beautiful man with delicate fingers and dark brown eyes. He was considered Arnold Rothstein's protégé, though Rothstein died of a bullet in the groin when David was fifteen. Rothstein had adopted him, and David went to "college" with the king of crime. Rothstein took him to the racetrack, to meetings with gamblers, to roadhouse gambling casinos, where David discovered his new "uncles," Legs Diamond and Frank Costello. With the aura of Rothstein around him, David had become a venture capitalist at sixteen, and the businesses he backed, like Joel's, never had any problems with labor racketeers and the law.

David loved to reminisce. He'd grown fond of Isaac, would let him ride his tiny knees, tell him stories about a Manhattan that Isaac could never have dreamed.

"It was Arnold who introduced me to the Ansonia. 'It's the only address worth having,' he said. Caruso lived there. Toscanini. Chaliapin. Babe Ruth. 'When I'm at the Ansonia,' he said, 'I don't ever want to go back out onto the street.'"

"But why didn't he live here?" Isaac asked.

"Please," Joel said, "don't pester David."

"It's a legitimate question. Arnold had a mistress on the thirteenth floor. Inez. He was crazy about her. What a creature. Tall and proud as a pelican. People would gawk at her when she took the elevator down to the swimming pool. Arnold had to hire a fiancé for her, or she would have had twenty marriage proposals a month. He'd plucked her out of the Ziegfeld Follies, a dancer with legs that shot to the sky. . . . "

"Mr. Pearl," Isaac muttered. "Inez's legs couldn't have locked him out of the Ansonia."

"Don't be fresh," Joel said. "You're interrupting David."

But the boy banker laughed, and then he started to cough. He was born with a weak heart.

"Look," Joel said, "you've aggravated him."

"Not at all. I enjoy Isaac's company. The kid is shrewd. He can visualize, see with his ears, like a detective. He understands the details. Inez was just *too* gorgeous. Arnold couldn't keep to the shadows with Inez around. He was a gambler, and gamblers have to hide. They have too many debts. The Ansonia had been one of his favorite haunts. But after he installed Inez, he had to give it up. 'David,' he said, 'it's a pity. Every time I'm on the stairs, with the wrought-iron rails, it's like having my own little piece of Europe. I never want to travel again.'"

The boy banker blew his nose with the help of a silk handkerchief, his initials sewn into the silk.

"Isaac, you can't imagine what the Ansonia meant to Arnold. It was like a love affair. He watched the building go up in 1901, watched it rise to seventeen stories, watched the stone masons work on the towers, when he was only a runt, a rich kid who despised other rich kids, and became a runner for Tammany Hall, a common cockroach."

"Rothstein a cockroach?" Joel mused. "Impossible."

"Arnold was at the opening ceremony. The Ansonia wasn't even finished. But its developer, Dodge Stokes, couldn't wait. He'd knocked down an orphan asylum to find a perfect site where he could build and build. And Arnold was there at this first, unofficial opening, with live seals swimming in the lobby fountain, and a tearoom that didn't have a single teacup. He was the representative of Big Tim Sullivan, boss of Tammany Hall. He recognized a couple of gamblers, but he didn't mingle with them. He tasted the punch and found the Ansonia's staircase, with its marble floor and iron grille, and he climbed all seventeen flights. And that's when he had his revelation. 'David,' he said, 'Dodge Stokes is a genius. He built Manhattan's first unsinkable ocean liner. It doesn't tilt with the wind. It sticks to its own street. But it leaves you with the impression of gliding along an invisible grid.'"

"Ah," said Joel, tipsy from the blue champagne. "Long live the Ansonia! But it's a shame I can't shake Arnold's hand. Didn't some stinking gambler gun him down in front of the Plaza?"

"The Park Central. And it wasn't really a gambler. It was the banks. Arnold had become a liability. He was too powerful. He'd funneled hard cash away from the biggest banks. He was prepared to ruin them, to form his own banking system with mob money. The bankers had to strike back. They hired the best gunman, a police captain who had a grudge. He cheated at poker, and Arnold tossed him out of the game."

"David," Joel said, "you're talking like a Marxist. Bankers don't send out killers. This is America. . . . What will Isaac think?"

"That the good *and* the bad die young. . . . Isaac, lose yourself, explore. The Ansonia is an entire territory. Your father and I have business to discuss. And it would bore you to death."

"But somebody could kidnap him if he strayed too far."

The boy banker looked into Joel's eyes. "Who would dare?" he asked.

And Isaac wandered around in his short pants. Ten years old. He'd never seen a circular living room like David's and windows made of etched glass. Joel's silent partner had been right. Isaac longed for details.

He walked out of the apartment, heard his father groan.

"I'm used up. . . . We never had to deal with gangsters. Not like this."

"Joel, welcome to the modern world."

"But a manufacturer who has to sit with hired gunmen so his workers won't strike . . . "

His father's groans gnawed at him, seemed to grate his own heart. He ran to the stairway, imagined himself as Rothstein visiting Inez. Each landing had a window that climbed to the top of the wall, and the whole landing was flooded with light. It was like being on a planet where the sun existed only to caress a boy in short pants.

And then, all of a sudden, the Ansonia fell out of his father's vocabulary. Joel stopped visiting his silent partner, could barely mention his name. "He's a crook, like his beloved Rothstein. And he'll end the same way. I don't want you near the Ansonia. David Pearl pollutes whatever he touches."

But Isaac wouldn't follow his father's instructions. He hiked from the Lower East Side to David's citadel, which seemed to dominate half the sky with its limestone skin.

"I'll live here," he said. "With Caruso's ghost."

He announced himself to the concierge, who stood behind a black marble desk that was like a many-sided maze.

"Mr. Pearl, please."

"Which one?"

"The man in the tower. David Pearl."

"And who should I say is calling?"

"His partner's son. Isaac Sidel."

The concierge was dubious of Isaac's credentials. But David sang his "OK" on the house telephone. "Maurice, let the kid upstairs. And don't give him a hard time. He's precious to me."

Isaac shunned the elevator. He took the magic stairwell, like a young mountain climber, caught in the windows' blaze.

The boy banker was waiting for him at the top of the stairs, and he himself was all ablaze, in a scarlet robe.

"I figured you'd climb. But I couldn't manage sixteen flights. I don't have enough air in my lungs."

He brought Isaac into his eagle's lair, fed him caviar and blue champagne.

"Any messages from your dad?"

"No, David."

"I see. You've come here without Joel's consent."

"I'm your silent partner," Isaac said.

"And what does our partnership consist of?"

"The past," Isaac said. "Papa doesn't have the time. Papa dreams of gloves. . . . Tell me about Arnold and the Ansonia."

"I've already told you."

"Tell me again."

And David relived the tale of Rothstein's arrival at the Ansonia in 1903 as a Tammany lout. Rothstein wore the colors of Big Tim Sullivan, a red blazer and an orange neckerchief. He'd come to the carriage porch without a carriage, pretended to step down from a horse. Big Tim had wrangled an invitation from the master builder Dodge Stokes. The mayor, Seth Low, was there, a big fat reformer with a walrus mustache, looking like the great French novelist Gustave Flaubert. Isaac had never heard of Flaubert.

"Idiot, he changed the whole landscape of the novel."

"I'm not interested in landscapes," Isaac said.

David laughed and continued with his tale. Seth Low had defeated Big Tim and the other bosses and chased "the Tammany tigers" out of City Hall. He'd resettled the orphans who lost their home when Dodge Stokes destroyed the asylum. He began building high schools in the poorest neighborhoods. He railed against the slums. He was the first honest mayor the town had had in years. And when he saw Rothstein's orange neckerchief, his jowls began to twitch. He demanded that Dodge Stokes kick out "this disgusting little tiger."

But Rothstein had his own razzle-dazzle. He bowed to Gustave Flaubert.

"Your Honor, I've contributed to your Homeless Orphans' Fund. Look it up. Rothstein. Twenty dollars. I'm your biggest fan among the tigers. Couldn't we get along? For one afternoon."

The mayor measured Rothstein's brown eyes. "Dear boy," he said. "I'll do anything, but take off that abominable scarf."

Rothstein obliged, and the mayor introduced him to Dodge Stokes and a certain Monsieur DuBoy, the French architect whom

Stokes had hired to build his Beaux-Arts palace. Rothstein mingled with them, drank punch, aware all the while that Tammany was working day and night to beg and steal the necessary "tickets" that would unseat Mayor Low.

"That's politics," Isaac said. "What about the seals?"

"Ah, the seals in the fountain. They had sleek, wet backs. But one of them escaped and bounced up the stairs to the Ansonia's tenth floor. It took nine policemen and the Central Park zookeeper to capture the seal, according to Arnold. But I wasn't there."

Isaac would have come every week to have his caviar and blue champagne. But on his sixth or seventh visit, he bumped into a catastrophe. Maurice, the concierge, told him that David Pearl had been snatched from his eagle's lair in handcuffs, charged with tax evasion, and that Isaac had better leave the premises or Maurice would have him arrested for vagrancy.

"I'm not a bum," Isaac said, but he went downtown where he had more grief. His dad slapped him and clutched his scalp. "Treasury men were here. They wanted to know how much money I was hiding for David Pearl. They'd already been to the shop, frightened my employees. And they were looking for you, my little Arnold Rothstein. I had to learn from them that you were running up to the Ansonia on the sly, sitting at David's feet. Did he stuff your pockets with cash?"

Joel had clumps of Isaac's hair in his hand. But Sophie Sidel arrived with a cigarette in her mouth. Isaac's mom looked adorable. She slapped at Joel with a broom.

"He's a criminal," Joel said.

"But he's *our* criminal," Sophie answered, the cigarette dancing with each stroke of the broom.

"I'll divorce you," Joel shouted.

"Be my guest."

And the battle ended right there. No Treasury agents arrived to question Isaac. David Pearl, Rothstein's heir apparent, was in all the newspapers. The mob's personal banker. The venture capitalist of crime. David was indicted, but he didn't have to sit very long in jail. His lawyer called him a philanthropist, the secret benefactor of a hundred hospitals and settlement houses. It was David Pearl who found a roof for every orphan whose home had been torn down by realtors like Dodge Stokes, David Pearl who sent kids from Harlem to a summer camp in the Catskills. No jury would convict him. The government's case was feeble compared to Pearl's largesse. He began receiving marriage proposals through the mail. He looked like Tyrone Power in his photographs. Manhattan's magnificent son. But he didn't return to the Ansonia. All the publicity had unsettled David. He vanished from Broadway. . . .

Joel didn't survive so well without his silent partner. He lost his government contract. Goons destroyed his shop. He lingered through the war, battling with Sophie. Then he also disappeared. Isaac and his younger brother, Leo, grew up without their dad. Leo became a kleptomaniac, and Isaac became a cop, so successful that he would soon be vice president.

4

SAAC CAMPED OUT AT GRACIE Mansion and kept a small apartment on Rivington Street, but the building had burnt down while he was campaigning. And Seligman decided that Citizen Sidel had to have his own headquarters and residence outside Gracie Mansion.

"It's a hornet's nest, Isaac. People will think you've living off the city's dime. Can't have Michael's VP eating up city resources. We'll rent a suite at Trump Tower where you and your team can entertain and do whatever you like."

Isaac groaned. He didn't have a team. He hated all the glass towers that had gone up after the war and had turned Manhattan into a monolithic forest. He'd have dynamited half the town if he'd been a dictator like Stalin.

"Then where would you like to live, sonny boy?"

And Isaac had a sudden mirage of a white castle rising out of the mist.

"The Ansonia," he said.

Tim grabbed the telephone, whispered for five minutes, winked at Isaac, and said, "It's a deal. I got you a sublet on the fifteenth floor."

"Timmy, I'm the mayor. I own New York. And you hop on the horn and get me into the Ansonia. Just like that."

"That old whore," he said. "The building's dilapidated. I wouldn't even put an enemy into the Ansonia, but you're our bohemian prince. The country loves you, Isaac."

Isaac wasn't listening. He had to defend the Ansonia, the one single landmark of his childhood. "Caruso lived there. And so did the Babe. Arnold Rothstein dreamt up his biggest gambling coups on the Ansonia's stairs."

"Ancient history," said Tim. "Rothstein's a dinosaur."

"He was the king of crime."

"Sounds like a comic book to me. I bow to the Party's new prince. Go on. Live at the Ansonia."

And Isaac did. The Secret Service moved Isaac into the Ansonia, and Martin Boyle had his men interview every single tenant.

"That's ungracious," Isaac said.

"Sir, it has to be done. We have to weed out the potential crazies, anyone who bears a grudge against you."

"And what happens if you find a couple of people like that?"

"Well, we give them a cash incentive to leave."

"And if that doesn't work?"

"We hound the hell out of them."

"Wait a minute. That's not legal, Boyle. We have rent laws in New York City. And I'm the guy who defends those laws."

"Then there's a conflict of interest. But I can't allow a crazy to live in the same building with you."

"Fine," Isaac said. "We'll have a lawsuit. The United States versus Citizen Sidel. . . . Boyle, it's my new home, and I don't want to be a pain in the ass. Kill the Gestapo tactics, understand?"

There were no crazies in the building other than Sidel, but on his very first day he found himself in the middle of a squall. There was a tenants' strike. The Ansonia was being converted into a condominium, and the building's new owner was putting pressure on tenants to get out. The owner lived in the building but wouldn't reveal himself. He was stockpiling vacant apartments, warehousing them. Yet Tim Seligman had sneaked Isaac into the Ansonia.

He had his bay windows, a bird's-eye view of Manhattan, his own nest. He would march up and down the stairs, which had grown shoddy and lost their shine, but Isaac could still bathe in the sun that broke through the enormous windows like great bells of light. He shivered with his own sense of the past, the recognition that this staircase in a rundown castle felt more familiar to him than his mansion in Carl Schurz Park or his boyhood home on West Broadway. And he understood why Arnold Rothstein had treasured it, why Caruso had practiced his arias on these stairs, why the Babe had swung an invisible bat in the stairwell's dreamy light.

It was a universe unto itself, forlorn, complete, with an astonishing silence where Isaac could listen to iron and glass and marble breathe.

He wished he could confront Maurice, the concierge from 1940 who'd been so rude to Isaac. He would have saluted this concierge in his military cap and frock coat, and said, "Maurice, now I know why you were so fucking fastidious. You were the Ansonia's watchdog, guarding its dignity, and I was an interloper, trying to crash the gate."

A little man came up to Isaac while he was playing Caruso, practicing his soliloquy on the stairs. But Isaac didn't have a chance to greet him. Martin Boyle jumped out onto the landing with a .22 Magnum and spoke into his button mike, "Possible flounder, possible flounder on the fifteenth floor."

"Jesus," Isaac said, "this isn't the Kremlin. Will you learn how to let go?"

He chased Boyle off the landing and twisted his body toward the man on the stairs. "I'm—"

"Citizen Sidel."

Even the Ansonia's incredible sunlight couldn't mask the little man's gray complexion and fishy eyes.

"The Democrats bought the building, didn't they?"

"I doubt it," Isaac said.

"Then who's been paying big bucks to get rid of us?"

"I'm not sure."

"The Citizen moves in, and soon we'll have a whole circus of Democrats. The Ansonia's your headquarters, isn't it?"

"On paper," Isaac said, "only on paper. I'm on the road a lot of the time, singing for my supper."

"That's cute, very cute."

The little man was clutching a pocket pistol, a .22 short. Isaac wondered if he'd ever been to San Antone, ever haunted the Alamo and that cattlemen's bar at the Menger. But Isaac didn't have his own star clerk inside the Ansonia to shove him out of harm's way. He almost missed Amanda Wilde.

"What's your name?" Isaac asked.

"The wife is sick. She has dizzy spells. I can't afford to take her to a heart doctor."

"What's your name?"

"Archibald Stearns."

Isaac had to be quick. He didn't want Martin Boyle to reappear with a gaggle of Secret Service men. Isaac would be stuck with a permanent shadow.

"Well, Archie, I'm the mayor, or did you forget? No one's gonna drive you out of the Ansonia. Trust me."

"Like I'd trust my mother," Archibald said, his fishy eyes wandering around with a rapid, lunatic rhythm. Isaac plucked the gun out of his hand and tossed it into the stairwell.

"That's better, Archie. Shouldn't point a gun. I'm only human."

Archibald Stearns ran down the stairs, and Isaac would have chased after him, but the sun got in his eyes, blinded him for an instant, and Stearns was already gone. Isaac went back to his apartment like a sleepwalker and said to his Secret Service man, "Call Columbia Presbyterian and ask for the biggest heart specialist. Have him come to the Ansonia."

"Are you having palpitations, sir?"

"No, no. It's not for me. It's for Archie's wife."

"Who's Archie?"

"The guy on the stairs. Archibald Stearns. Find out where he lives . . . in the Ansonia. And charge the doctor's visit to my election fund."

Isaac dismissed Boyle and got Seligman on the horn. "Tim, will you tell me who owns this goddamn white elephant, huh?"

"An admirer."

"That's grand. Will ya give me his name?"

"I can't disclose that. I'm sworn to secrecy. But he's contributed to your campaign in a big way."

"Then Archie's right," Isaac muttered. "I am driving people out of the Ansonia. I am the villain of this little piece. . . . Do I have to start digging, Tim? I'll find the fucker and break his neck. Should I call the *Village Voice*, tell them that the Democratic National Committee is pro-landlord? That will really make us the hit of Manhattan."

"Isaac, I still can't deliver him. But if you're that suicidal, we might as well let the Prez piss in the Rose Garden forever. Good-bye."

Isaac had a dead phone in his fist. Fuck the Democrats. He'd have to do a little "detecting" at the Ansonia, but where to begin? And then he noticed an envelope on his desk. It contained the lease for subtenant Isaac Sidel, c/o the Democratic National Committee and a certain Inez Corporation. Isaac was a dope. *Inez.* Rothstein's beautiful blond mistress with legs as silky as an ostrich feather. David Pearl hadn't fled the Ansonia. He'd exiled himself to his eagle's roost on the sixteenth floor.

Isaac climbed up one flight, slid along the Ansonia's carpets, and knocked on David's door. But he'd misfired. An opera singer now lived in David's old roost. And by chance, on a sudden whim, he climbed up to the seventeenth floor. The maids of rich men had once been shelved here. That's what David had told him. The ceilings were low, the rooms were tiny, and comprised a labyrinth of cubicles, a rat's maze.

Isaac could only find one door. He wasn't shy.

"Open," he said. "I have my lock picks, David. And I could ask the Secret Service to lend me a battering ram."

"Who is it?" someone growled from inside the door.

"The Citizen. Isaac Sidel."

"Are you still wearing short pants?"

"I've outgrown them lately."

The door opened, and Isaac recognized David Pearl's big brown eyes. The boy banker hadn't aged, like the Citizen himself. His hair was white, but his beautiful features hadn't coarsened a bit. Isaac perused David's labyrinth—the tiny, rattish rooms, cluttered with cardboard boxes and books. Isaac had to duck his head before he could enter. That's how low the ceilings were. He felt like some loutish Gulliver in the land of the small.

"Why did you move into this maze?" Isaac growled.

"It fits my temperament. I'm a recluse."

Isaac glared at him.

"How's your heart, David?"

"Beats like the devil."

"When did you buy the building?"

"Years and years ago."

"Was it your own homage to Rothstein?"

"I'm not that sentimental. I got it at a steal."

"Then why the Inez Corporation?"

"It was a perfect cover," David said. "Who else but the Ansonia's historian would have remembered Inez's name?"

"I'm not the Ansonia's historian."

"Yes, you are," David said. "I saw it in your fucking eyes almost fifty years ago. You were hooked. The building was like your own magic mirror. You went right through the looking glass, and you've never climbed out."

"Mirrors and mirages," Isaac said. "But at least I saw a little of the planet. You've been like a privileged tramp in a limestone castle. Do you ever go out for coffee?"

UNDER THE EYE OF GOD

"Why, when all the coffee in the world can come to me."

"What forced you into exile, David? The humiliation of a judge and jury?"

"Not at all. I was holding too many markers. A lot of bankers were in my debt. They decided to get rid of me in an easy way. They snitched to Uncle Sam and the IRS. Tax evasion. When I'd helped those sons of bitches hide their own cash. But they hadn't counted on Manhattan's crazy venue. I had my own mirrors and mirages. I played the sly philanthropist."

"And you won, David."

"It didn't matter. I'd been betrayed. I called in every marker. I ruined the men who tried to ruin me."

"Like the Count of Monte Cristo. And you sit in your jail."

"Jail, Isaac? The Ansonia's hardly a jail. I lost my taste for mercantilism."

"But you could have traveled."

"How? To be a common tourist and salaam in front of the Eiffel Tower and Big Ben? I had the Ansonia. That was enough. I followed your career. You're like one of my orphans. I helped where I could."

Isaac was gloomier than ever. He didn't like the *thread* of this conversation.

"Helped?"

"How does a policeman rise and rise? With baksheesh."

"You bribed City Hall and the goddamn NYPD?"

"I didn't have to. I contributed to the Fresh Air Fund, let a particular cardinal know that the Irish mafia who ran the police had to make room for Isaac Sidel."

"It isn't fair," Isaac said. "I'd still be a cop on the beat if it hadn't been for you."

"No. I feathered your way a little. You had the goods. A kind of honest cruelty."

Honest cruelty. The wizard in his labyrinth had Isaac's number.

"Should I dance for you, David?"

"I don't expect any favors from Citizen Sidel."

"You just happened to lend the Ansonia to the Democrats, huh?"

"Did you look at your lease? Seligman is paying through the nose."

"And why are you warehousing apartments?"

"I'm waiting for the market to rise. There's nothing sinister about it."

"But I met a man on the stairs. His wife is sick. . . . "

The telephone rang. It was Martin Boyle. He'd tracked Isaac to the seventeenth floor.

"Sir, I went through the building's directory. There's no Archibald Stearns at the Ansonia."

"Boyle," Isaac said, "I'll be with you in a minute." He hung up the phone. "A little man with fishy eyes. Swore he was a tenant. Archie Stearns. His wife has heart problems."

The ex–boy banker started to laugh. "Was he packing a tiny pistol? Isaac, you're lucky to be alive. He's no tenant of mine. He's a hired gun. Dennis Cohen. Works for my competitors, a gang of real estate moguls who'd like to grab the Ansonia. He's dangerous, Dennis is."

"Dennis the Menace."

"He's waiting for me to come out onto the stairs."

"But he could have knocked you down if he really wanted to," said Sidel.

"That's not Dennis' style. He was Frank Costello's bodyguard once upon a time. But Costello wouldn't adopt a Jewish kid from the Lower East Side. Dennis was always on the outside. He had to freelance. I used his services on a couple of occasions."

"Then why is he coming after you?"

"I told you. He's a freelancer. A hired gun. He'll sit and wait. Dennis has all the time in the world."

"Not with me in the house. I'll bring you his scalp."

"Isaac, I'm fond of Dennis. We have a history together. Like me and you."

Isaac returned to the landing, found Martin Boyle.

"Sir, we checked. The mystery man is Dennis Cohen. He's a tough cookie, with three or four convictions. I had to call the Bureau."

Isaac groaned. "Is the Bull coming here with one of his joint task forces?"

Isaac was feuding with the FBI and its director, Bull Latham. "What if I went after Dennis myself?"

"Then I'd have to cover you and forget all the other rules."

"Come on. Help me find Dennis."

"Sir, we know where he is. Our boy's in the attic.

"He isn't a boy," Isaac said. "Show some respect."

David wasn't alone in his labyrinth near the roof. They found an opening in the hallway, climbed a flight of winding stairs and, for a moment, Isaac had a touch of vertigo, thought he was rocking on the sea. Ah, David's castle was an ocean liner, after all. Boyle snapped the chain on a narrow door with a pair of wire clippers. They ducked their heads and dove through the door. Isaac's vertigo was gone. They'd entered an unbelievable country. The attic was stuffed with debris and ancient artifacts. Mirrors that had lost their silver backing, sideboards that had begun to peel, a chipped water fountain that must have been home to the Ansonia's seals. They'd come to the land of mirrors and mirages, and Isaac envied David all of a sudden. That realtor with the white hair had a richer life than the Citizen, with all the brouhaha of a mayor and a Commish.

"Boyle, let's get out of here. This is a holy place."

"It's an attic, sir. And Bull Latham is right behind us. He'll get the glory when his marksmen shoot Dennis down like a dog."

"But I want to capture him . . . alive. He's practically a landsman of mine."

"I saw his chart, sir. He's zapped entire families. He's . . . "

Something stirred among the debris. A rat scattered between Isaac's legs. He looked up. Dennis Cohen was in the rafters, right above Isaac, his .22 short aimed at Boyle's heart. Isaac didn't think, didn't measure Boyle's life against a gunman's. He glocked Dennis

Cohen, shot him six times, and Dennis nosedived, crashed into a mirror, created an enormous sprinkle of glass . . .

■ ■ ■

ISAAC AVOIDED BULL LATHAM, LEFT the Ansonia with the Secret Service. Dennis Cohen was carted to the morgue. There were pictures of Isaac and the dead gunman in every paper on the planet. Isaac's face was more familiar than Caruso's had ever been. The Democrats' capital began to rise again. But nothing could soothe the Citizen. He belonged in the attic, with all the debris. He'd have tossed the vice presidency into a garbage can, if he could have been at the Ansonia in 1903 and watched those seals swim. He'd killed his brother, Dennis Cohen. Isaac had to sit shivah for Dennis, do his seven days of mourning.

He sat on an old wooden crate, in a ripped overcoat, the visible sign of his grief. Rothko's overcoat, he mumbled to himself. The telephone rang on his second day of mourning. Martin Boyle picked up the phone.

"It's your astrologer, sir."

"Tell her to soak her head."

"She says it's urgent, Mr. President."

Isaac grabbed the receiver. "Amanda darling, are you going to sing me a lullaby about the stars?"

"I'd rather sing about Dennis Cohen. I was fond of that little man."

"You met Cohen? Where? When?"

"At the White House."

Isaac groaned. "He worked for Calder?"

"Occasionally."

"Jesus, it's Billy Bob Archer all over again. I ought to move into the Menger Hotel."

"It might be safer than a birdcage on Broadway."

"What birdcage?"

"The Ansonia," she said. "Are you wearing your Glock?"

"How can I? I'm in mourning," Isaac said.

"I didn't really call about Cohen. I have a new job. . . . I babysit for Marianna Storm."

"Where is she?" Isaac asked.

"Right here."

Marianna crept onto the line.

"I miss you, Uncle Isaac. *Monstrously*."

The Big Guy sobbed in his torn coat.

"Couldn't we meet, Marianna? I'll wear a disguise."

"And wreck your future? . . . I'm Lolita, the little firebomb. I can't even bake you a batch of cookies. Mr. Seligman says people might call it provocative. You aren't wounded, are you?"

"No. I wasn't even scratched. Marianna . . . "

"We won't be able to talk until January. This is the last time."

Marianna abandoned Isaac. He sat there on his wooden crate in Rothko's overcoat, grieving for Dennis Cohen . . . and Citizen Sidel.

PART TWO

5

HE WAS IN HIS OWN strange kind of limbo, no longer quite the mayor and not much of a vice president–elect. Tim Seligman didn't want him near the Waldorf, near J. Michael or the Little First Lady, Marianna Storm. He felt much closer to the Prez. Both of them were in love with Margaret Tolstoy, that orphan from Odessa who'd drifted into Isaac's junior high school class dressed in rags, half a million years ago, and had intoxicated Isaac with her almond eyes. She'd been trained in a KGB kindergarten, and now worked for Bull Latham at the Bureau. She also protected the Prez and was his personal Scheherazade, who entertained him with tales about her and Isaac Sidel. But no one could be on Calder's safe side. He'd nearly gotten her killed, and she lay in a coma for two weeks. The Big Guy blamed himself. If he hadn't attached himself to the Democratic ticket, it might never have happened.

Isaac had to cast about in the Bureau's own waters to find her. She was in one of Bull Latham's "blinds," a clandestine nursing home in the woods of Upper Manhattan, near the Cloisters and Fort Tryon Park. This home didn't even have a name. It's where the

Bull delivered his most important agents to mend. Sometimes they didn't mend at all. And they lived out the rest of their lives in this little cloister.

He panicked that Margaret might never really recover, and that she would be mummified in Upper Manhattan at Bull Latham's retreat, like a home for retired nuns. He had the devil of a time getting in. The nurses all wore guns. But they recognized Sidel and didn't want to buck a future vice president. Margaret had her own room. It was as lavish as the Waldorf and looked out upon the Jersey cliffs. She was already mummified, with a bandage around her head. Her almond eyes gazed at Isaac, took all of him in. She smiled, as if she'd met some wild and woolly stranger.

"Have you come to give me a bath?"

He started to blubber, with the Glock still in his pants.

"Don't cry," she said in the sweetest voice. And Margaret had never once been sweet. She held his hand. And that's when Bull Latham ventured into the room, with all the bravado of a linebacker who had once played for the Dallas Cowboys. His aura was as great as Isaac Sidel's. The head of the Bureau wasn't a rattlesnake, like J. Edgar Hoover had been. He wasn't a poisonous man with manicured nails. He didn't rant about the reds. He had a Texas drawl, even though he'd come from Minneapolis. If Calder had dropped Teddy Neems, his bagman of a vice president, and picked the Bull, he might have won. At least it would have been a contest, with Isaac debating Bull Latham, another guy with a gun in his pants.

"Your Honor," he said, "she can't recognize you. . . . I've tried. Margaret thinks I'm her butler or something. It breaks my heart."

Margaret sat up in bed with her bandage. She flirted with the pair of bandits beside her. "My two boys," she cooed. She was still holding Isaac's hand.

"I'll wait outside," the Bull said.

Isaac adored every vein on her arm, every pucker where some needle had pierced the skin. She released the Big Guy's hand and started to remove her hospital gown. "Darling," she said, "you can't give me a sponge bath without a sponge."

He had to wind her back into her gown. Her beautiful white hair had begun to grow wild. She was much lovelier without a wig, and Margaret had always worn wigs, as she romanced some gangster for the FBI. She'd lost her childhood somewhere in Odessa, had been a courtesan at twelve, a secret agent at thirteen. Her life had been carved out of one brutal void after the other.

He stroked her arm with the bumpy cusp of his hand, the lord and master of a sponge bath without a sponge. She closed her eyes and fell back onto her pillow. He didn't have the heart to banter with her. He tiptoed out of her room. The nurses had never seen a vice president–elect with tears in his eyes.

The Bull lent Isaac his own handkerchief. They'd been battling for almost a year.

"Bull, did your fingers ever break?"

"What?" Bull Latham asked.

"When you were with the Cowboys, did they ever break? You don't have a linebacker's hands. They seem much too delicate."

"I had to tape them all the time . . . but it's not the hands that give you trouble. It's the knees. They're a linebacker's nightmare. That's why I had to leave the Cowboys. If I'd remained another year, I would have become a gimp."

"I want to visit her without notice," Isaac said.

"Understood."

"And I don't want any interference from the Prez."

"You have my guarantee. Calder won't bother you."

"If I have an urge in the middle of the night . . . "

"Every door will be open for you," the Bull said. "You shouldn't have shot up Dennis Cohen."

"Come on, he was Calder's man. He would have been an embarrassment. He's more valuable to you dead than alive. And I didn't have a choice. He was going to put out Martin Boyle's lights."

"But you could have winged him."

"Not a chance," Isaac said. "He was Frank Costello's own gunman. He would have gotten off a shot. And I'd have had to sit shivah for Martin Boyle."

"But Boyle isn't Jewish."

"I'd still have to mourn him, wouldn't I?"

And Isaac left that clandestine place near the Cloisters. The vice president–elect didn't have much of a future without Margaret. Nor did he have much of a past. All he had left was Arnold Rothstein's favorite building in Manhattan. And he marched down to the Ansonia from Fort Tryon Park.

6

THE BIG GUY COULD HAVE carried all fifty states on his back, won Mars and the moon, but J. Michael was flawed beyond repair, and it had nothing to do with his alcoholic wife. The kid was Isaac's own creation. He'd been a student radical at Columbia in '68, and Isaac had kept him out of jail. J. was almost a sharecropper. Both his parents had been kindergarten teachers in the South and had to break their humps to put food on the table. But Michael had risen up like some proletariat Monte Cristo to become the players' chief representative in the middle of a wildcat strike. He made the owners eat crow. Baseball had never had its own czar until J. Michael Storm, who could ride right over the commissioner and presidents of both leagues. He'd shuttled between Manhattan and Houston, where he had his law firm and was registered to vote. Clarice had been a gray-eyed beauty from Abilene before she became a guzzler. She was seventeen when he plucked her out of a fancy finishing school and married her. And now Michael lived at the Waldorf, which had once been Jack Kennedy's home away from the White House. J. wore sunglasses, like Jack, had mistresses in every corner, but he didn't have Jack's aristocratic veneer and magical looks. He had kindergartens in his blood, not Hyannis Port. Poor J. had to invent himself.

He wasn't much of a mogul. He went deep into the wilds of the Bronx and purchased parcels of land with a rickety enterprise called Sidereal Ventures. He wanted his own empire near Yankee Stadium after he rescued baseball from a crippling war. But Sidereal was rife with illegal land grabs. On paper, it owned a quarter of the Bronx, but no one had been able to figure who ran Sidereal, certainly not its principal officers, Michael and Clarice.

J. had almost been indicted in Miami for another one of his deals. And prosecutors all over the country wanted to bring down the president-elect. It was Calder who kept him alive, Calder who had Justice hide J. Michael within its own muzzle. Tim Seligman was blackmailing the Prez. The Dems had pictures of Calder with his prick out in the Rose Garden. And Tim wouldn't even discuss whatever else he had on the Prez. But Justice could no longer protect Michael. Prosecutors had begun to bark for his blood.

Sidereal was on the front page of the *Times*. The *New York Post* called J. Michael the emperor of the Bronx. There were rumblings in the *Milwaukee Sentinel* and the *St. Louis Post-Dispatch*, talk of a constitutional crisis. If J. Michael was indicted, what would happen to the presidential process? The Electoral College could vote for Mickey Mouse.

Still, Michael soldiered on at the Waldorf, behaved like the president-elect, while Tim Seligman fumed and tore at his own scalp. Isaac himself was banned from the Waldorf. Party chiefs didn't want the Big Guy to show his face. He could provoke the crisis. How could he replace Michael *before* the Electoral College met? Suddenly, the election itself was a wisp in the wind. And so Party theoreticians scribbled for a week, and Michael held a press conference in the Grand Ballroom at the Waldorf, with Clarice and the Little First Lady at his side. No one bothered about Clarice, but reporters shivered at Marianna's poise and the green of her eyes. They were electrified before Michael spoke a word.

"I may have gone too far," he said, "but I wanted to rebuild the Bronx. And so I had to play the emperor, as some reporters have said. But I didn't make a dime from Sidereal—in fact, it ate up whatever cash I had. But I'd wander half a mile from Yankee Stadium and see a wasteland that left me numb. Torched buildings and mounds of rubble on both sides of the Cross Bronx, a borough ruined by a mad highway right down the middle of its spine. For the Bronx and its residents, it will always be a highway to nowhere. And so I was rash, ladies and gentlemen. I pushed too hard, and my accounting wasn't always correct. But I had to push, or nothing would ever have been done."

The reporters and Democrats in the ballroom were delighted with Michael's little war cry. But they kept asking about the Big Guy while they purred at Marianna.

"Mr. President, why isn't the mayor here with you?"

Michael smiled and spun closer to the Little First Lady. "Don't jinx me. I'm only president-elect. And I didn't want to intrude upon the mayor's time. He has to run this town and prepare for the vice presidency. And Isaac has a will of his own. That's why we love him."

"But didn't he rescue you once, sir, while you were a student radical at Columbia?"

Michael leaned toward the gallery of reporters like some coconspirator. "He didn't rescue me. He saved my life. I wouldn't be here with you if he hadn't knocked some sense into me. That's why I had to have him on the ticket. If I'm rash again, he'll knock some sense into me for the next eight years."

The reporters clapped, but they wouldn't let him off the podium without questioning the Little First Lady.

"Miss Storm, is it true that you have a swain of your own, a little bandit from the Bronx?"

There was blood in Marianna's eyes, but she didn't want to ruin her father's press conference, so she held back her rage.

"Angel Carpenteros isn't a bandit. He's an artist and a Merliner, like me. He decorates the walls of broken buildings. But he had to move upstate."

Angel had commemorated the fallen warriors of the Bronx's worst gangs, but he'd also been a rat for the NYPD; everyone wanted Angel dead—the cops, the gangs, and probably the Democrats, who couldn't afford to have him involved in the Little First Lady's affairs. If he'd gone back to Spofford, the Bronx's notorious jail for juveniles, his throat would have been cut within a week. So Isaac hid him upstate. He had brought Angel into the Merliners and then whisked him away.

But the reporters didn't know that much about Angel Carpenteros. Suddenly, they had Shakespeare in Manhattan, Romeo and Juliet in the South Bronx. There'd been no daughter of a president-elect quite like Marianna Storm. They could imagine all the other swains she'd have in DC. They have enough copy for a lifetime.

"Miss Storm, Miss Storm, what will you do on your first day in the White House?"

"Run to Uncle Isaac's office in the West Wing with a batch of butternut cookies. He can barely survive without them. And I'll have to alert the White House cook. I'm mistress of whatever kitchen I enter. Papa's new mansion won't make much of a difference."

Everyone was excited again about the White House of J. Michael Storm. But Clarice bristled in front of the reporters. She'd worn her silver lamé dress, could have been Manhattan's own Cleopatra, and not a soul in the ballroom glanced at her. Reporters heard Clarice mutter "little bitch" under her breath. But she couldn't ruin Michael's press conference. She'd never capture the imagination of America. She was part of Michael's entourage, that's all. America had a new First Lady, and it wasn't Clarice.

■ ■ ■

THE DEMS CONSIDERED MICHAEL'S PERFORMANCE a masterpiece. Their man had triumphed, but the Big Guy wasn't so sure. *Something stinks,* he muttered to himself. Isaac wondered if a smokescreen was coming directly from the White House. Justice had J. Michael dancing on a stick, and somebody would have to fall. He had his own mavens at Finance rifle through their dossier on Sidereal Ventures, but there were no officers listed other than Michael, Clarice, and the Little First Lady. Sidereal wasn't in arrears; it paid all its tax bills on time.

But who had asked little Dennis to smoke Isaac *after* the election? Somehow, it was tied up with Sidereal, with Michael's own dealings. And what about Billy Bob, the maniac in San Antone? That little adventure in the cattlemen's bar was disguised as a deep Texas plot of far right fanatics. Another smokescreen. And what did Calder have to gain? Isaac was about to dial the White House. But the world had its own fucking magic. The mayor's phone rang in his empty office at the Ansonia. It sounded like the scream of a bat.

The Prez himself was on the horn. "Isaac, I'm in the neighborhood. Can you meet me at Carl Schurz Park in half an hour?"

"Calder, why Carl Schurz Park?"

"I just landed on your lawn."

Calder wouldn't let J. Michael steal Manhattan from him; election or no election, he was still the Prez. And he'd been hovering over the town on board *Marine One*, after a dash to the Rockaways and Jones Beach; his one pinch of popularity was in the outer boroughs. And Isaac had to race up to Gracie Mansion with Calder's Secret Service. The Prez was still inside his chopper, a hundred yards from the mayor's mansion; *Marine One* had the nose of an eagle.

Isaac had to have special clearance before he could climb aboard; one of the Prez's own wild boys patted him down. He had to leave his Glock outside the bird. The inside of *Marine One* was like the bedroom of a trailer, with leather cushions and a rocking chair. Calder was wearing a Stetson and boots from Abilene. He was born and raised in Arizona, but he'd modeled himself after Lyndon Johnson, the most tenacious and successful senator the southland had ever had. Like Lyndon, Cottonwood was a very tall man. He'd come roaring out of the Senate with Lyndon's own panache. He'd grab you by the lapels, the way Lyndon would, and lift you right up to his nose. It didn't matter to him that Lyndon was a Democrat and a damn New Dealer. He could spit at you like a snake. And Texas had always been his buffer. It was another country, where men and boys carried guns and would ride two hundred miles for a steak. It had its own music, its own literature, its own profound civility. It was no accident that the official residence of Calder and J. Michael was Houston. It had become America's new center of gravity.

Calder couldn't even stand in his own castle. He was nearly eight feet tall in his Stetson, and he would have been inches from the roof of *Marine One*. His boots were hand-carved, a gift from Lady Bird Johnson. He felt like a stranger on Pennsylvania Avenue, in a town that couldn't even make a decent po'boy or a quesadilla. He'd had to fire half a dozen chefs. He insisted that Isaac drink a root beer with him.

"Mr. President, what the fuck is going on? You could have crucified J., and you're letting him waltz right into the White House."

"J. is nothing. You're the man I feared."

"Come on," Isaac said, trying not to belch from the root beer. "The Bull could have hammered me into oblivion. I've killed people, I've been in bed with the Maf."

"But folks love that. It's the Wild West. Besides, you're a poor man. I had the Treasury boys check your bank account. Isaac, you'll have to feed on ham sandwiches for the rest of your life. You give your money away to beggars and children in baseball caps."

"Then how come you tried to have me whacked?"

Calder wasn't even embarrassed. He'd sent half a dozen hitters after Isaac during the campaign, and all of them failed.

"Son, I was jealous, filled with bile— Isaac, if you're wearing a wire, I'll kill you right in this tent."

"Jesus," Isaac said, "your own desperados patted me down and took my Glock. I'm naked without it."

Calder began to cry. "I had the Bull put Margaret in that nursing home. Did she recognize you? I visited with her this afternoon. That's why I'm here. I choppered right down on the roof of her sanitarium. I held her hand. She looked in my eyes and called me Mr. Death. What kind of name is that?"

"I won't discuss Margaret with you," Isaac said.

"Then what else do we have to discuss?"

"Billy Bob Archer and Dennis Cohen."

The Prez seemed hurt by Isaac's remark. "I didn't hire those shooters. Lord, the election is over and done."

"But Amanda Wilde says that Dennis Cohen once worked for you?"

"And you believed that whore? . . . I did have him on the payroll. But that was a while ago. Besides, I enjoy jousting with you. J.'s a sissy, a lawyer in knee pants who represents millionaire baseball players."

"Did Dennis work for Sidereal?"

Calder barked like a seal, but it didn't sound like the laugh of a sane man. "We all work for Sidereal."

"Yeah," Isaac said, "and I suppose we're all star clerks. But Sidereal isn't in the stars. It's eating up the Bronx, block by block."

"That's J.'s business, not mine."

"J. doesn't know shit. He and Clarice are a couple of clerks."

Something was bothering the Prez, or he wouldn't have bothered to whirl out of the sky and sit on Isaac's lawn at Carl Schurz Park. The visit itself was a smokescreen. Calder was frightened of a Bronx corporation that had never even earned a dime. Sidereal. Was Houston money behind the whole plot? Was there some sun god hovering over the Houston Ship Channel with a morbid interest in the Bronx? And had that sun god himself dispatched Calder Cottonwood? The Prez had visited the badlands of the Bronx three times this year. And it couldn't have been part of his strategy to lure the Latino vote. The Latinos flocked to J., who posed with Puerto Rican and Dominican baseball stars. No, that Texan in the tall hat had been scouring the badlands for something else.

"Mr. President, help me, please. Who the fuck are you afraid of?"

"Son," Calder said, "I'm afraid of God and the devil, just like everybody else."

Something still bothered the Big Guy. *Sidereal, Sidereal.*

"Calder, did you send a bunch of army engineers into Claremont Park to survey the badlands of the Bronx?"

The Prez wrinkled his nose. "Isaac, I've never been near an army surveyor in my life."

He snapped his fingers once and turned away from Sidel, who was tossed out of *Marine One* and landed on his ass. And before Isaac could blink, the blades began to whirl and Calder rose into the sky again. Winter dust flew across the lawn. And Isaac felt like some embittered child, beaten in a game he'd never get.

7

THE BIG GUY NO LONGER cared what embargoes had been placed upon him. He ran to Clarice's apartment on Sutton Place South. Marianna's own Secret Service man, Joe Montaigne, wasn't that eager to let him in. Montaigne was a sharpshooter from Missouri who could have shot out Isaac's lights.

"Jesus, Joe, I'm not here to see the Little First Lady. I need Marianna's nurse."

"She doesn't have a nurse," said Joe Montaigne.

"Then her shopping companion, her diction coach—Amanda Wilde."

Clarice was in the living room with an enormous tumbler of Scotch. She was shivering, and Isaac had to take the tumbler out of her hand.

"Fuck J.," she said. "Fuck the White House. J. can live there with that little bitch. I'm not moving out of Manhattan."

"Ah, Clarice," the Big Guy said. "It's the media. Those mothers are the real ghouls. Once you occupy the White House, they'll be mad about you."

"Shut up," she said. Her gray eyes had gone all glassy. She fell into Isaac's arms, and he sat her down on the sofa, while Marianna spied at him from her own playroom, which was larger than the flat Isaac had once had on Rivington Street. Like some blond femme fatale with a little baby fat, she was wearing lipstick and mascara at twelve. Marianna could throw him into immediate despair. She herself had a wistful look, but Isaac wouldn't give her a chance to say a word.

"I didn't break our pact. I'm here to see the star clerk—Amanda Wilde."

And then Amanda appeared; she was no longer roly-poly. She wore lipstick, like Marianna, and was dressed in a perversely seductive black. The Little First Lady must have groomed her. Isaac clutched the star clerk and went out on the terrace with her.

"Amanda, I'm in the dark. What the hell is Calder afraid of? Why does he hover over Manhattan on *Marine One*?"

"He isn't hovering," she said. "He's marking time."

"I'm slow," Isaac said. "I don't get it. He has to bump around in the sky?"

"He's waiting for Cassandra's Wall to open."

Isaac was more confused than ever. "What is Cassandra's Wall?"

"A very exclusive private club. Even Calder had a hard time getting in. He's still on probation."

"The president of the United States has to audition for a club like some college freshman? He's the one who can kick ass. Cassandra's Wall should be auditioning for him. But how come I never heard of it? I'm the mayor."

"Mayors don't count," she said. And Isaac was more aggrieved than ever.

"I'll close it down."

"You couldn't get near Cassandra's Wall . . . without an escort."

Amanda winked at him. They went back inside the apartment, where Amanda found a sleek winter cape she must have borrowed from Marianna or Clarice. Isaac was wearing a World War II infantryman's foul-weather coat that he'd swiped from a barrel on Orchard Street. The Big Guy was always searching for bargains. He looked like a refugee from a Manhattan gulag. Amanda went to hug Marianna.

"Baby, I'll be back."

"You needn't rush," Marianna said, wiggling out of Amanda's embrace. "I'll have some whiskey with Clarice."

"Don't you dare," the star clerk said, and began to giggle on the elevator. But she stopped giggling when she saw Martin Boyle in Isaac's sedan.

"You can't take him with us to Cassandra's Wall. The Secret Service isn't allowed inside."

"Mr. President," Boyle said, ruffling his Oklahoman's nose. "What is Cassandra's Wall? It isn't on our itinerary. I'll have to search the premises."

"Boyle," Isaac said. "I'm on a caper. You'll spoil my fun. . . . I'll wear my button mike. You can knock the door down if I'm in trouble."

■ ■ ■

ISAAC GREW BITTER WHEN HE discovered the home of Cassandra's Wall. It was right in the basement of the Ansonia, where Plato's Retreat had once been, and before that the Continental Baths. Isaac had crusaded against the porno mills and sex clubs, and had shut down Plato's Retreat, the most extravagant of all the clubs, a bathhouse and bordello where most of the "whores" were dentists' wives from New Jersey.

The Big Guy was outraged. "The bathhouse reopens and no one bothers to tell me? I'll murder all my building inspectors."

But Isaac remembered the Ansonia's basement before it housed the Continental Baths or Plato's Retreat. It was a swimming hole for retirees when Isaac had visited David Pearl as a woolly boy from the Lower East Side. Part of the basement had also been a Ping-Pong club, when Ping-Pong was a sport to be reckoned with, and there were tournaments in every town across America. Manhattan had its own young champions, Marty Reisman and Dick Miles, who dominated the sport and played epic three-hour matches in Madison Square Garden, held Ping-Pong aficionados in their thrall. And David would accompany Isaac into the bowels of the Ansonia, where Isaac could watch distinguished old men paddle around in bathrobes at their private Polar Bear Club, then turn left, into a ragged Ping-Pong parlor, right under the Ansonia's steam pipes. David himself would commandeer Reisman, demand a twenty-point spot in a game of twenty-one points, hurl a hundred dollars under the table, clutch his racquet with the stubbornness of a demented man, and lose all the time, while Reisman stood in a red gypsy shirt, with very wide sleeves, and flicked the ball back at David. He was like some half-blind avatar in thick eyeglasses, but Marty Reisman didn't even have to look at the table. He could attack David's shots with his eyes closed, hit the ball from some perch behind his back, and still spot David twenty points.

"My kid," David said, even though he wasn't that much older than Marty Reisman. Years later, when Isaac studied the life of that other half-blind avatar, James Joyce, at Columbia College, he always thought of Reisman. Both of them had a sense of purity about their craft, both of them flourished with their fragile eyes.

But Isaac wasn't in much of a mood to be nostalgic. He realized now why Cassandra's Wall wasn't in the city's books. It wasn't even registered as a club. It had no real address. It was part of David's Beaux-Arts colossus, the Ansonia. He went into the bowels of the building with Amanda Wilde. No one frisked him at the door; no one bothered about his Glock. That was the mystique of Cassandra's Wall. It only existed for its patrons. David hadn't even supplied it with much of a lock.

There were no refreshments, and there wasn't even a side bar. Its cavernous halls still had the debris of Plato's Retreat, a mattress room where all the swingers congregated, where all the wives were swapped. It had the blue light of a bordello.

"Amanda, what's going down here, huh? Is this the devil's monastery?"

"Shh," she said. "Cassandra's Wall is where the richest men in the world come to gamble."

"That's ridiculous," Isaac said. "I know all the richest men in the world. They're real estate moguls. They live in Manhattan."

"Isaac," she said, "these realtors of yours, they're only pretenders to the throne."

And she led Isaac into a very dark room that didn't have the same garish blue light. There were five men and a woman who stood in a tiny circle, chatting among themselves. The woman had a raucous laugh. She was wearing a backless blue dress; Isaac could see the lovely nodules of her spine, even in that unreliable light. She had a helmet of silver hair, and when she turned to face Isaac, the Big Guy's knees began to wobble. She had a beauty that was beyond Isaac's comprehension. Her face didn't have one classic feature. Her nose was a little too long, her forehead a little too high, her brown eyes a little too far apart. But when she smiled, all the features fell into line, and her face was on fire.

Amanda introduced him to the five men, reclusive billionaires from the Old World; one was an Italian aristocrat who lived off his family's accumulations; another was a French financier who had something to do with cement; the third was a Russian oil bandit who had a monopoly on railroad cars; the fourth was a chocolate magnate from Belgium; the fifth was a German publisher who owned companies everywhere. They were all polite to the Big Guy but had never heard of the vice president–elect. Mayor Sidel hadn't even entered their mythology. He couldn't remember their names. Claudio? Ivan? Igor?

But the woman's face was still on fire. She must have been thirty or thirty-five. Isaac began to stutter.

"Your n-n-n-name?"

"Inez."

And suddenly, Isaac felt murderous, as if he were part of some random kindergarten class and had been tricked and pummeled by his own teacher. *Inez.* Arnold Rothstein was alive and well . . . and living in the Ansonia.

He didn't bother to chat her up. He bowed to all the billionaires and left Cassandra's Wall without Amanda Wilde.

8

HE CLIMBED UPSTAIRS TO DAVID Pearl's own retreat on the seventeenth floor. He had to wonder why the ex–boy banker would live in a labyrinth with low ceilings when he could have had a lavish piece of the castle all to himself. The Big Guy didn't even knock. David was sitting on his window seat in a worn sweater. He wasn't surprised to see Isaac.

"Dennis hadn't come to the Ansonia to kill you, David. He was your very own gunsel."

David smiled his wizard's smile. "Indeed. Frank Costello lent him to me—the most loyal kid I ever had."

"Jesus, Dennis was a grandpa. He was growing senile. He would have had to wear diapers all over again. Why did you send him after me?"

David whistled under his breath. "He would have nicked your arm, that's all."

"He was aiming for Martin Boyle's heart."

"I don't have a moratorium on Secret Service men. They're Calder's peons."

Isaac saw blue spots in front of his eyes. He wanted to strangle

David, crack him open on his window seat. His own mentor, David Pearl, his *muse,* had been stringing him along.

"And Billy Bob Archer, did you hire him, too?"

"Sort of," David said. "He was put there to shake you up, not kill you."

"I suppose I'm your indispensable man."

David laughed with that childish face of his. He hadn't aged much in his castle. He had that same devilish enthusiasm he'd had when Isaac first met him. "You're dear to me—part of my little family."

"And is Amanda Wilde part of your family, too?"

"You could say that. She was my private secretary, still is."

"But hasn't she wandered rather far afield?"

"No, I catapulted her right into the election process . . . let her become the president's astrologer—and mistress."

"And is the president your own personal peon?"

Isaac was mortified. Had he been one of David's peons from the moment his father had introduced them, almost fifty years ago?

"Isaac, you give me a little too much credit. I'm one lone bachelor with a dinosaur of a building."

"Stop it," Isaac said. "Calder is scared shitless of you . . . and so is J., I suspect. You're the man behind Sidereal."

David clapped his very delicate hands; the sound was like an echo from another world. "Bravo," he said. "I buy up properties, and I sit on them. I never, never sell."

"How much of the Bronx do you own?"

David picked at his scalp like some man in the middle of a brainstorm.

"You'd have to ask Amanda. She's the one who keeps count. . . . I would say at least half."

Isaac could have been sitting with Dr. Mabuse, the mad emperor of the underworld, or with another mad emperor, like Merlin. But this Merlin was a recluse *and* a landlord.

"And did your own minions torch the Bronx?"

The emperor smiled. "Some of them did, but I purchased most of the properties after they were torched."

"And what could you possibly gain?" Isaac asked. "The Bronx will never come back. It's been dying for thirty years."

"Isaac, Isaac, that's just a pinch of time. You have to think in centuries if you want to rebuild a borough."

"But, David," Isaac pleaded. "You won't be here."

"That's not the point. You can't create an empire on mortality charts. My strategy is crisp as a church bell. One day, Sidereal Ventures will tear down the Cross Bronx Express and build a highway under the ground. And I won't put up a maze of shopping malls and warehouses in the old, deserted lots near the Cross Bronx. We'll have brand-new neighborhoods."

Isaac began to wail. "Why couldn't you have told me? I would have helped you swallow up Robert Moses' fucking tunnel in the sky."

"Ah," David said. "But not with Sidereal's help. And I would have had to step out of the shadows. It was much too risky. I'll stay where I am."

That wizard with the narrow chest was the reincarnation of Rothstein. He was Manhattan's new king of crime. The first AR sat with senators. His whisper went all the way to the White House. He could buy an apartment on Park Avenue, which had a covenant against Jews. Rothstein could bankroll any operation, legal or not. He'd had gambling dens, had owned a piece of the New York Giants, had invested in Broadway shows. That's how he must have discovered Inez.

"David, are you as secretive as AR?"

The wizard smiled again. "Arnold wasn't secretive enough. That's how he got killed. Half the planet knew his steps. He had his own table at Lindy's, sat there like a clerk. How many times did I meet him there, while he was writing up the day's receipts on a lick of paper? He would send me out on errands. I'd deliver thirty thousand dollars in a paper sack to some politician or police chief. . . . "

"But why didn't you tell me you had your own Inez?"

Isaac had startled the wizard, caught him in a snare. "I don't visit graveyards, Isaac. Inez is under the ground."

"But I just said hello to her . . . at Cassandra's Wall. She has her own helmet of silver hair."

The wizard's worry lines disappeared. "Ah, *that* Inez. She comes with the furniture. She's a tart."

"But she didn't seem out of place with a little band of billionaires."

"A tart," David muttered again. "I found her, groomed her, gave her the clothes on her back."

"Then why is she with those billionaires?"

"Why else? To distract them, to eat out their hearts . . . your lady with the silver hair is my secret agent."

Isaac didn't believe the wizard. "What's her real name?"

"Trudy Winckleman. She was the sensation at a cathouse in Detroit— Isaac, you need all the edge you can when you're betting a hundred million on one shot."

Was Manhattan's king of crime also an imbecile? Wouldn't those other billionaires have perverted his plans and plied Ms. Trudy Winckleman with hard cash? But Isaac didn't like David's tricky smile.

"Did you know that AR once bet half a mil on one toss of a coin? He had to line his pockets with thousand-dollar bills. And he was always broke. He had betting fever.

He'd watch a cockroach climb up a wall and have to bet on its progress. He'd bet on a ball game. . . . "

"Isn't he the man who fixed the World Series of 1919?"

"A fishwives' tale," David said. "Gamblers bribed ballplayers in Arnold's name. He had nothing to do with the fix. I wanted to sue fucking F. Scott Fitzgerald while he was still alive. He defamed Arnold, turned him into Meyer Wolfshein, a greenhorn with a forest of hair in his nose. AR had the softest voice. He spoke like a duke. He was much more elegant than an Irish scribbler from St. Paul."

Isaac adored *The Great Gatsby* and Fitzgerald's portrait of Meyer

Wolfsheim, who understood that the world couldn't thrive without some business "gonnegtion."

"David, what was your hundred-million-dollar bet about?"

The wizard began to purr. "What else? The presidential election of '88."

All of Isaac's goodwill was gone. He wanted to rip off David's scalp.

"You bet against the Democrats, didn't you?"

"Kid, I've always been in your camp."

Isaac cursed himself. He didn't need Cassandra's Wall to tell him what was going down. David had bet on him, and him alone, bet that Isaac would be the new president, not J. Michael Storm. All the rumblings in the press had started from the Ansonia's seventeenth floor.

"You fucker," Isaac said. "You're betting that Michael will take a fall."

"Like Humpty Dumpty," David said. "But Calder won't be there to pick up the pieces. You'll inherit the White House from him."

"And what if I don't let it happen?"

"Ah," David said. "Play Cassandra. Be my guest. I'll double my bet."

"I could run to Tim Seligman," Isaac said.

"And have him sink his own Party? Not a chance. Tim will behave."

"Then I'll shove Teddy Neems into the top spot. I'll give all the marbles to Calder's own vice president."

"Teddy's my bagman. He'll do whatever I say.. . . Isaac, you can run around like a renegade, shoot up half of Manhattan with your Glock, and you'll still be Prez."

"And my first act as president will be to fry your ass. . . . David, tell me, where does Trudy Winckleman live?"

Isaac was already defeated. It was Manhattan, where any hunter could become the hunted in a matter of minutes.

"Where else?" David said. "At the Ansonia. In Inez's old apartment. It's poetic justice. I put her where AR kept his own true love. Did you know that Inez died in my arms? I didn't abandon her after Arnold was killed. She always went to bed with AR's picture under her pillow. She could have gone back to dancing, joined some revue.

I told her it wasn't dignified. I paid her bills. We had tea every afternoon. . . . "

Isaac grew delirious with David's recollection of Inez. Most of his rancor was gone. He was in love with the first Inez and the second. David had kept Inez's apartment intact, not as a museum, but as a devotional, with cherry wood dressers, an armoire, a mirror that had once belonged to Lillie Langtry . . .

Isaac's head swam with all the details. David didn't have to tell him where Trudy Winckleman's apartment was. Like most gamblers, AR had suffered from triskaidekaphobia, a morbid fear of the number thirteen. But he'd tried to wean himself away from that fear, according to David. So he parked Inez on the thirteenth floor. She griped and griped, but Arnold wouldn't relent. He had to place his own mistress and himself in jeopardy. It titillated him.

Isaac didn't care. *Triskaidekaphobia*, he muttered to himself and ran out of David's labyrinth.

9

THE BIG GUY WASN'T BASHFUL. He knocked on Inez's door. No one answered, and he wondered if she was still in the bowels of the Ansonia with her billionaires. And just when he was about to give up, she came to the door in an old cashmere bathrobe that must have belonged to Arnold Rothstein's original lady. Her smile hurt the hell out of Isaac.

"Mr. Mayor," she said in that raucous voice he remembered from Cassandra's Wall. "Did you want to play cops and robbers? Are you here to frisk me? Come in."

It was a museum, no matter what David said. The drapes seemed out of another century. There was a photo of AR and Inez on the mantle in Trudy Winckleman's elongated living room. AR seemed a little coarse in the photo; he didn't have the beauty that Isaac liked to imagine for him. His mouth was too large, his forehead too broad, his eyes a little too far apart. But Inez had a voluptuous, staggering blondness. She stared out at Isaac like the most brazen of girls. She must have been a handful for AR. Did she flirt with Babe Ruth? Did she conspire with other kept creatures in the building? Flo Ziegfeld had his mistress on one floor, his wife on another. God knows the damage Inez must have done.

Trudy Winckleman caught him looking at the picture. She was as bold as Inez in her helmet of silver hair.

"Mr. Mayor, would you like to move in?"

Suddenly, Isaac began to fumble with his words. "Miss W-w-winckleman," he muttered.

"Call me Inez. Everybody does. What did that madman upstairs tell you about me?"

"Said he snatched you out of a bordello in Detroit. But I didn't believe him."

"Darling, don't apologize for David. Like everything he says, it's half true. It was New Orleans, not Detroit. But I didn't work on my back. Sometimes I wish I had. I was the accountant for a string of very fashionable whorehouses in the Garden District and a single mother with two kids. One of the clients mistook me for a whore—offered me thousands to live with him in New York."

"Was it David?"

"Of course not," she said. "David never travels. It takes a whole army to deliver him to Wall Street once or twice a year. My new beau was a banker, nowhere as rich as David. With a wife and kids in the suburbs. He paid me more than I could have earned in a year."

"But how did you meet David?" Isaac asked, not even sure he wanted to know the truth.

"In the Ansonia," she said. "That's where my banker found an apartment for me. But he was a very tiresome man—jealous and stupid. He stole back all the money he had put in my account. I was left stranded. I couldn't pay the rent. But I wasn't thrown out. And that's when the madman appeared in his flea-bitten sweater. He said I could have an apartment rent-free on the thirteenth floor. And he had a proposition."

"He wanted you to play Inez."

"Isaac dear, it isn't easy. I feel like a relic. And David doesn't even traffic me around. I mingle with his gambler friends, but not as their personal siren. I'm not at their beck and call."

"And your two kids?"

"Both at a private school in Connecticut. The madman pays the bills. I visit them as often as I can. I keep a small apartment near the school. I wouldn't want them to see me here. I'm not allowed to disturb a picture on the wall."

"Then why do you stay?"

"Habit, I suppose. And laziness. And the power I have over men. I'm an icon. How can I fail? Isaac, be a darling and take me for a stroll."

Inez preferred the loneliness of Riverside Park. There were no picnickers or jugglers or panhandlers, just a few old men practicing their golf strokes on the bumpy hills and the secretive men and women who kept their boats in the marina. The trees were all barren in early December; the ground was strewn with dead leaves that had begun to turn into dark red dust. It was Isaac's favorite time of year, when the park was mostly devoid of people. He and Inez had a long, narrow kingdom to themselves.

The wind blew right at them, and Isaac draped Inez in the folds of his foul-weather coat. His blood began to heat up at the nearness of her. He was already unfaithful to Margaret Tolstoy, who lay near the Cloisters, her mind half gone. Why was he always running after some femme fatale?

He was the knight-protector of fallen ladies. Inez shivered under Isaac's rough material.

"Darling," she whispered, "you'd better watch out. David is betting that you won't live very long."

"Ah," Isaac said, "he's my mentor." His knees were shaking, and it had nothing to do with the wizard on the seventeenth floor. He wasn't thinking of politics, or of Marianna's sea-green eyes. He had a vision of that bleak landscape near the Cross Bronx Express, the gutted buildings, mile after mile of debris, and he remembered how comfortable he was amid all the rubble. It was home to him. And Inez could have risen out of that rubble.

They kissed. Her tongue tasted of almonds. It was sweeter than his own life. He was already devoted to this gorgeous masque, who had to hide within another woman's history, live among her expensive ruins. But something had startled her. She broke from Isaac's embrace.

He turned around, looked into the barren trees. Martin Boyle was standing there, clutching a Mossberg Mountaineer with a sniper scope.

"Jesus, did you have to follow me into the park with a fucking deer rifle?"

"I'm sorry, Mr. President, but I was following whoever followed you."

"What are you talking about? Can't you see? I'm with Inez."

Boyle tried not to glimpse at Inez's helmet of hair.

"Sir, the shooter was standing behind a tree. . . . Your brains would have been scattered in another minute."

"Enough," Isaac said. "Where is this shooter of yours?"

"He got away. I couldn't track him. I thought . . . "

"And he left his calling card. A Mossberg Mountaineer."

Inez was much more civil than the Big Guy. She shook Boyle's hand, thanked him for saving Isaac's life. Boyle had been bitten by her, too. He blushed when she slid her hand out of his. Isaac wondered to himself—two Adams and their Eve.

They walked out of the park together, while Isaac's Secret Service man still held that deer slayer in his arms.

■ ■ ■

SHE HAD TO GET RID of Isaac. Inez, or whoever she was that afternoon, feigned a headache. She kissed him between the eyes, as if she were aiming some bullet, and ran upstairs to her retreat on the thirteenth floor. Why did she always have to get involved with desperados? No one had to whisper in her ear that Isaac was a doomed man.

She'd have to get out of Manhattan. She wasn't going to be David Pearl's Cassandra. But she didn't have any of her clothes in this rotten tomb with windows. Trudy Winckleman was the phantom, not Inez—Inez had a bureau, photographs on the wall, boas from the Ziegfeld Follies, satin panties, and the sheerest gowns in the world.

She puffed on a cigarette from one of Inez's pearl and silver holders. She didn't have to wait very long. The old man had come downstairs in the velvet slippers of a billionaire who was loathe to leave his labyrinth.

"Fuck you," she said. "And fuck all your plans. I'm not staying."

He started to shiver. She knew that the first Inez had often blown her fuse. And no one could contain her, not Arnold Rothstein or David Pearl.

"Davey," she cooed, because that's what the other Inez had called him. "What if I fall in love with the big dope?"

"Ah, that would be a pity," said the billionaire—she'd heard the rumor that he owned more real estate than the Rockefellers, that his holdings could dwarf any empire.

"Isaac's lovable, but you'd better hold the line."

"And what if I can't? He's wooing me, for Christ's sake."

"A lot of men have tried to woo you, and they haven't gotten into your pants."

"And what if I wanted to let him into Inez's pants? Because I don't have a single pair of my own."

"That would be a catastrophe."

"Were you really going to shoot his head off, Davey? You should have warned me that I was going on a death march in the park."

"And if I'd warned you?" David Pearl asked like some menacing beggar boy.

"I would have taken him into some hollow and kissed him for half an hour . . . to warm him up for the kill."

He started to cackle. She pulled his ears, and he really was a beggar boy, Inez's beggar boy.

"Davey, if you come downstairs again without knocking on Inez's door, I'll take your whole head into my mouth and you'll never get it back."

He shuddered with terror and delight.

"You'll woo the big dope, but my way."

And he paddled out of the museum in his slippers.

PART THREE

10

THE DEMOCRATS WERE FRIGHTENED TO death of leaks. A phantom shooter in Riverside Park? The vice president–elect with a mystery woman who was connected to Arnold Rothstein's own phantom lady? It was too much for Tim Seligman to bear. Isaac couldn't be seen in public with this bitch in a silver helmet, not until Michael's coronation. Meanwhile the owner of the Mossberg Mountaineer was tracked to a hunting lodge in Montana. The deer slayer had been reported stolen a month ago. The owner himself was a registered Democrat who had voted for Storm-Sidel. He couldn't have been the phantom shooter. He was at his hunting lodge on the day the shooter had stalked Sidel.

There wasn't a word about it in the press. But Michael himself wasn't so lucky. Another one of his mistresses had surfaced with her own tattletale in the *National Enquirer*. Democrats called her a Republican plant . . . and a slut.

Meanwhile Isaac busied himself. He'd been an absentee mayor for months, but his aides ran City Hall without him. He went into Manhattan's deeds and records with his property clerk and discovered that the Inez Corporation and its affiliates owned more buildings and lofts in Manhattan than Columbia University and the Catholic Church. But David hadn't lied to him. Inez never sold a piece of property. It held whatever it had. And its properties wove from the tip of Manhattan to the edge of Spuyten Duyvil Creek. The little wizard had to be wealthier than John Jacob Astor, Manhattan's first real estate baron. And still he sat in the Ansonia, like some forgotten man.

Was it AR himself who had sent him on a quest to buy up as much of Manhattan as he could? The Inez Corporation owned entire blocks. It had secret fiefdoms in Fort George and Washington Heights. But Isaac still wasn't satisfied. He ventured into the Bronx with his Secret Service man, looked down upon the ruins from that same hill in Claremont Park where he had spotted the army engineers. And he had his own sudden illumination. There was a certain symmetry to the widening swaths of waste. The torchings that helped break the Bronx weren't as random as they seemed. Isaac could have been looking down into the gigantic bowl of God's own football field.

And while he pondered in Claremont Park, Bull Latham arrived without his usual contingent of FBI men. He'd strayed far from his habitual watering hole in Manhattan, the Bull & Bear, a stockbrokers' bar and restaurant within the Waldorf. He wore a Siberian coat of white fur with all the elegance and grace of a movie star.

"Mr. Mayor," he said. "I'm not here. You've never seen me."

"I know," Isaac said with the same complicity. "You're at the Bull and Bear . . . and I'll pay particular attention to what you never told me."

"Exactly," the Bull said, while Isaac motioned for Martin Boyle to move out of earshot and he turned off his own button mike. Only God or the devil could have listened in.

"Bull, there's a pattern out there in that heart of darkness down the hill."

"Mr. Mayor, I've been thinking much the same thing. . . . It's like driving Indians off the reservation."

"And then putting up a new reservation without the Indians."

"Think Pentagon," Bull said. "That's what this land grab is all about."

Isaac began to shiver—suddenly, the surveyors and engineers made a lot of sense.

"I suppose there's a new Peter Minuit . . . and he's buying up bits and pieces. He'll make a killing on this reservation. Will it be a missile training site?"

"Nothing as fancy as that," said the Bull. "Just a military base that will stretch across the southern half of the Bronx, below the Grand Concourse. The Pentagon wouldn't want to mess with the New York Yankees. Its generals will let the Bronx Bombers have their castle and some room to breathe. Wouldn't want the stadium to be an isolated island. But the man who leases or sells this Indian country will make a fortune beyond our own ability to imagine. He has to be stopped."

"But can you pin him to any crime?"

"Probably not. But he's had people killed. I'd be willing to bet that the shooter in San Antone was attached to the Pentagon in some weird way. And Mr. David Pearl means to stifle you."

"But he's my mentor," Isaac groaned. "I learned about the city at his feet. He's a disciple of Arnold Rothstein, did you know that?"

"Rothstein wasn't half as ruthless. It's your being mayor that worries him, not presidential politics. Vice presidents can't harm him, but a mayor can."

"But until a month ago I thought he'd vanished without a trace."

"Isaac, if you found him, it's because he wanted to be found."

The Big Guy wished now that he'd never been tagged as J. Michael's VP. He could control Party politics in Manhattan and the Bronx. But even Staten Island scared him a little. It had too many hills, and its politicians were too much a part of the American mainland. Cottonwood had squeaked past Storm-Sidel and had taken Staten Island by a hair—517 votes. Rothstein's protégé, David Pearl, wanted to bump Isaac upstairs. The Big Guy was embarrassed to talk about his brand-new sweetheart, Inez, who guarded David's reliquary at the Ansonia. But the Bull mentioned her before Isaac had the chance.

"Careful, Mr. Mayor. We have photos of you kissing Mata Hari in the park. She's poison. She seduces businessmen for that little potentate, turns them into swine."

Isaac was heartsick. "Never mind her. What about the shooter with the deer rifle? Do ya have any photos of him?"

"We don't need any photos. He was just a kid that David hired, a delivery boy with a stolen gun. I'm not even sure he knows how to shoot. We snatched him right away. But he lawyered up and I had to let him go, or I'll have the Civil Liberties Union hot on my tail."

Martin Boyle wandered over to Isaac and Bull Latham.

"Sir, Tim Seligman is on the horn. He says it's urgent. He wants you downtown—at the Waldorf."

The Bull barely hid his smile. "Good," he said. "Then I can bum a ride with you guys . . .where would we be without the Waldorf?"

11

THE BIG GUY WAS FRIGHTENED to death of the DNC. He'd rather have faced the Inquisition. He could talk to Tim, could deal with Tim's strategies, but not the little gang behind him—the lawyers and politicos who picked presidents and also sank them. They'd pulled Michael out of obscurity, and were probably planning to dump him. They choreographed the Democratic Convention, decided on the Party's new stars. They were the ones who saw Marianna's possibilities with the media and decided to lock Clarice away somewhere. The president could only have one First Lady.

And so he had to meet with the seven grand inquisitors of the Democratic National Committee, plus their spokesman Tim. There wasn't a smile or hint of recognition among them. They'd stolen out of Washington, DC, and descended upon the Waldorf, having laid siege to the president-elect until Michael was almost a prisoner in his rooms. But they wouldn't greet Sidel in one of the Waldorf's public salons. They'd turned the election into a holy war; and a holy war could only be battled out in secret.

The seven grand inquisitors had secured General Douglas

MacArthur's old suite in the Waldorf Towers. MacArthur had been a Democrat, and a holy warrior, who had napalmed North Korea and wanted to bomb the Chinese back into the Stone Age. These inquisitors sat with their stone faces in MacArthur's drawing room. They were worried that J. Michael wouldn't last, that he would fold before the Electoral College convened, and that could provoke a crisis.

The DNC's legal wizards had already met and declared that Cottonwood couldn't hide behind the Constitution, couldn't demand another election, since the Constitution was silent about a disappearing Democrat who happened to be the president-elect. The country had had its say. And it was up to the winning Party to pick a new team at the helm. Isaac had all the validity of the election process. He would move into Michael's slot, and now these inquisitors had to scratch their heads and find another vice president. The Party wanted a senator or governor from the southland to balance Isaac's New York credentials. Scared as he was, Isaac told the inquisitors to stuff themselves.

"I won't run with any cracker," he said.

Tim Seligman began to sway like some mystical rabbi. "Isaac, Isaac, we have to create a new ticket."

"Then go with someone else. I'll step away."

"Impossible," said Ramona Dazzle, the DNC's own chief counsel. "We'll lose all our credibility, and Cottonwood will creep right back into the process."

"It's worse than that," said Tim. "The Electoral College could revolt. . . . There will be faithless electors all over the place."

Isaac couldn't understand all this mumbo jumbo; the inquisitors had a votive talk of their own—technical *and* bewitched.

"Jesus, Tim, will you speak my fucking language?"

Ramona Dazzle glared at Isaac. A Rhodes scholar from Stanford, she sat at the pinnacle of the Democrats' brain trust and was the fiercest of all the inquisitors. Very few lawyers dared confront her in open court. She was like a gorgeous cybernetics machine. She had big brown eyes, sandy hair, and the thinnest nostrils in the world.

"Sidel, are you insane? If you abandon us, the electors will do whatever they want. And then a Republican Congress will declare Cottonwood the winner by default and hand him a second term."

"All right," Tim said, "we'll play hardball with this prick. . . . Sidel, who the hell do you want? Give us five choices."

"I only have one," Isaac said. "Bull Latham."

A strange calm had descended upon the Democrats. And then there was a collective groan. Isaac could have sworn that General MacArthur's ghost had come into the room.

"The Bull's a diehard Republican," Ramona shouted from her seat.

"The better for us in a constitutional crisis," said Sidel.

The seven inquisitors gaped at Isaac, meaning to drive him out of MacArthur's drawing room with stony stares. But Isaac never winced. Suddenly they realized that there might be an eighth inquisitor in the room—Isaac Sidel. And they began to listen.

"A fusion ticket," he said. "The country will go for it. And the Republicans won't dare rebel, not with one of their own on our team."

"But will the Bull come into our camp?" Ramona asked, her big brown eyes darting everywhere at once.

"I'll offer him a sweetheart deal," Isaac said with a smile that was at least as cryptic as their own icy demean.

"But the Bull can hurt us," Ramona said. "What if he doesn't sever his links with the FBI?"

Isaac glanced at her across the table. "Ramona, tell me what powers the vice president has?"

"None," she said. "He has to nurse his own dick. But I still don't like it."

"Then convince Michael to stay."

"He's collapsed on us," said Tim. "He sits in the dark and cries. He won't meet with his transition team. It's a disaster."

"Then who's your man?" Isaac asked. The inquisitors couldn't even look into Isaac's eyes. He'd pummeled them by riding right over their own little Inquisition. "Who's your man?"

"Isaac Sidel," said the DNC.

"I'll have Michael back in harness for you. Just give me an hour."

And he rushed out of General MacArthur's suite.

12

THERE HAD ALWAYS BEEN AN air of abandon about him. As a young inspector in the NYPD, he'd taken his daughter, Marilyn, into a hoodlum's bar on the Lower East Side. It was filled with remnants of Murder, Inc. Marilyn was four at the time. And the bar's resident gangster, Melvin Warsaw, hated the sight of young girls. He promised that he'd demolish every cop's daughter who wandered into his territories and would eat her alive. Isaac couldn't tolerate such a challenge to his own esteem.

Like a crazy man, he ventured into the bar with Marilyn riding on his shoulders.

She was wearing a white dress, like some half Jewish saint. Warsaw closed his eyes, and his cheeks grew purple with rage. "I can sniff Isaac Sidel. Mister, you brought your little girl here at your own peril. Little girls remind me of the misery of my own life. Sidel, I'll give you a second chance. Run away from here."

"Not until you shake my daughter's hand."

The whole bar was stupefied. Isaac went up to Warsaw with the little girl right under the chandeliers. She was singing to herself.

But suddenly she looked into Warsaw's eyes. She held out her hand to him, and Melvin Warsaw of Murder, Inc. was caught within her sway. He began to sob.

"Whoever harms this little girl will hear from me."

Marilyn had a new godfather, and Melvin became Isaac's stoolie for the rest of his natural life. The Big Guy was just as reckless with J. Michael. Student radicals at Columbia had wanted to bury Isaac in the catacombs of Hamilton Hall. But he walked through their barricades with his badge pinned to his coat in the spring of '68, talked Marx and Hegel and Ho Chi Minh with the radicals and was able to arrange a truce with their leader, Michael Storm. . . .

He had to pick the lock on the front door of Michael's suite. The president-elect was lying in his underpants on the Waldorf's king-size bed. He was muttering to himself, *"It's no use, it's no use."*

The Big Guy didn't turn on any of the lights. He let J. Michael continue with his mourner's kaddish. And the moment Michael turned silent, that was when Isaac pounced.

"Fine," he said, hurling Michael off the bed in his underpants. "Don't think that David Pearl and his friends at the Pentagon are going to grant you immunity. I'll prosecute the shit out of you the moment I'm Prez. I'll have my attorney general chase you under the ground."

J. Michael blinked at Isaac from his perch on the floor. "You can't shove me like that. I'm the president-elect."

"Not if you run away from your own election—Michael, be a mensch. What the fuck do they have on you?"

"Everything. Old man Pearl has me by the balls. I signed documents . . . I had buildings torched in Sidereal's name. For the good of the borough, Isaac. I thought they were going to build a new Yankee Stadium in the middle of Crotona Park. It would have revived the whole South Bronx."

"And you would have been the savior—our little Joan of Arc. They're not reviving the Bronx, Michael. They're gonna kill it."

"I know."

J. Michael crawled toward the Big Guy, his buttocks in the air, like a wandering turret.

"Isaac, he has the president eating out of his hand. Cottonwood can't take a leak without a nod from Pearl. That's why he pissed in the Rose Garden—he was so fuckin' distraught."

"And you?"

Michael began to blubber. "I can't fight him. He has too big a net. It's all run out of Texas—Houston and San Antone."

The Big Guy's ears perked like a deranged rabbit. The cattlemen's bar at the Menger had been no divine accident.

"What's in San Antone?"

"Brooks Air Force Base and Fort Sam Houston. They have their own little conclaves all over the map. New Mexico, Florida, California . . . and Texas."

"But David Pearl never travels. He doesn't stray from the Ansonia's seventeenth floor. He's like a monk."

And now Michael's own smile was deranged. "Monks don't have to travel. The military have their own mystical flying machines. . . . Isaac, I want out."

"Have you met Trudy Winckleman?"

"David's mistress, you mean."

Isaac's heart squeezed like a merciless ventilator. He had to sit down on David's bed. No wonder she was such a museum piece. Why shouldn't the wizard claim his own Inez? And Isaac was the fool of fools. One kiss and he was willing to protect Trudy Winckleman against the whole planet. It was Isaac who needed protection.

"Michael," he said, "don't give up. While I'm still mayor, that old man doesn't have shit. I'll dismantle him, I promise. He's not turning the Bronx into a military utopia."

"And what if he dismantles me first? Each fuckin' day there's another revelation, another misdeed in the sorry life of Mr. Michael Storm."

"They still can't bring you down. We walloped the Republicans in forty-seven states. Trust me."

JEROME CHARYN

And Isaac raced out of Michael's suite like an antelope. He returned to his headquarters at the Ansonia. *Headquarters*. It was the wizard's lair, not his own. David ruled the Ansonia, but he didn't rule New York, not while the Big Guy was mayor. He went upstairs to David's little labyrinth. A woman opened the door. She had the wizard's own sweet face. She was a distant cousin of David's who'd fallen on hard times and was his housekeeper.

"But where's Mr. Pearl?" Isaac asked, with a glum look. This cousin had recognized the mayor of Manhattan. Isaac had to give her his autograph on a napkin.

"I have no idea," she said, and she couldn't even tell him when David would be back.

"Mr. Mayor," she said, "don't forget the handicapped when you get to the White House." And she revealed her own withered left arm.

"But I won't get near the White House," he said, "except for an office in the West Wing that's just for decoration. Vice presidents have little to do."

She must have been her own clairvoyant. "Michael Storm's a crook. He won't last in the White House one week."

Jesus, everybody was jinxing him. He preferred to have a vacation at the Naval Observatory, where vice presidents had their own little nest. Isaac could catch up on his sleep. He dreaded his next move, but he still strode downstairs to Inez. Would she lie in his face, swear that she wasn't the old man's sweetheart? Suddenly, David wasn't so old. The Big Guy himself wasn't that far away from collecting Social Security. It would save his skin. He was always broke by the end of the month.

He was trembling by the time he reached Trudy Winckleman's door. She didn't answer any of his knocks.

"Inez," he muttered, "it's me."

He was filled with spite—cuckolded before he even slept with Inez. He took out his lock picks and entered that little museum. It had a fragrance—a sudden perfume—that walloped the Big Guy, barely left him standing on his own two feet. *Inez's aroma*. The world

84

would always remain a mystery to Isaac Sidel. This calendar girl, this fraudulent Inez, was enough to derail a guy. He had no scruples. Margaret Tolstoy was lying like a mummy in Bull Latham's sanitarium, and all he could think about was this delicious spider with her silver hair, woven right out of David's web.

He wasn't a burglar. He wouldn't go through Inez's drawers. He looked at that picture of Arnold Rothstein and the first Inez on the museum's mantelpiece. AR seemed more authentic than his protégé. He didn't have David's angelic mask. And AR's Inez wasn't cluttered in mystery. She was a showgirl who had caught Arnold's eye. But she didn't preside over a club for billionaires.

Then the Big Guy had another revelation. There was no billionaires' club. Cassandra's Wall was just a phantom, meant to suck in Sidel. He abandoned Inez's aromas and went into the bowels of the Ansonia. He broke into the place. It was utterly deserted. There were no signs of a human habitat. Rats scurried across the old mattress room of Plato's Retreat. The baths were bone dry. Isaac went out onto the street. He wanted to howl his own lament. But he cried somewhere deep inside his own bowels. The Big Guy was sitting shivah for himself.

PART FOUR

13

I T MUST HAVE BEEN 1924. The busses were as tall as skyscrapers. A sedan could seat nine or ten passengers. There was a bit of wonder on every block. Manhattan had become the new colossus. The cafeterias were flooded with dancers on a little break from some rooftop restaurant, and they all crowded into Lindy's for a glimpse of AR or their favorite bootlegger. It was a long, narrow delicatessen right on Broadway. No one could reserve a table except AR himself—it was near the window, and one of Arnold's enemies could have shattered the glass shooting at him. But no one dared. It would have been like shooting some deity.

The boy sat at Arnold's feet, worshipped the fluff on his collar. Little David and the Jewish Goliath. AR had had an older brother, Harry, whom his father adored. Harry had been a scholar, a religious Jew, and Arnold had always been an outcast. He preferred the downtown gambling dens. His father was a millionaire from Bessarabia, a manufacturer of cotton goods who kept synagogues and religious schools afloat. There was peace at home while Harry was alive. But Harry died of pneumonia before he was twenty-one. And AR blamed himself, swore he had willed Harry's death.

He became more and more of a lone wolf. He gambled, bought up properties while he was still in his teens. David himself was eight or nine years old when he chanced upon AR at Lindy's delicatessen. And Arnold was a man of forty-two, half worn out. There was little luster in his eyes. He had a gorgeous blond wife at home, and she threatened to leave him unless he dropped his "whore" at the Ansonia. But AR was addicted to Inez.

David was at the delicatessen with his dad, a clerk in a department store who idolized AR and sent his son over for an autograph. Arnold stared at David with his habitual melancholy.

"What is it you want from me?" AR asked in that musical voice of his—and when David had to think back at that moment, had to recollect, it seemed that Rothstein resembled J. D. Salinger, not that sinister greenhorn, Meyer Wolfsheim—Salinger and AR had the saddest eyes in the world. At least that's what he thought when he discovered a photo of Salinger many years later. *Lord, he looks just like AR.*

But he was getting ahead of his own story. David looked into Arnold Rothstein's lonely eyes.

"What would you like from me, little man?" Arnold asked again.

"A job," David said.

Arnold didn't laugh at a nine-year-old boy. He listened to every proposal, and he had more than a thousand proposals a day.

"What can you do?"

"Protect your life."

And now Arnold did have to laugh, but not out of disrespect. He liked the little boy's pluck.

"But I already have Legs Diamond as my own little man."

David knew all about Legs. Gangsters had become as popular as baseball players. Legs was always in the news, dodging bullets like some ballet dancer.

"AR, I wasn't thinking of any gunsel. Legs is crazy, and I'm not. But Legs can't keep a secret, and I can. He's always showing off to his girlfriends."

"And what kind of secret could you hold for me? I'm here at Lindy's every afternoon, prompt as a church bell."

"The secret of your accounts," said the boy. "If money has to be moved, I'm the man to move it. And how could I ever hope to trick you, AR? Legs would kidnap my dad, for God's sake, or do worse."

AR hired him on the spot. Of course, David's dad never knew a word of their deal. David would come to the delicatessen after school, sit at Arnold's table like a little scholar. And he wouldn't accept a dime.

"I'm your apprentice," David said. "And apprentices should never be paid."

"Why not?"

"It makes them greedy—and disloyal. David Pearl can't be bought."

He was soon invaluable to AR; he could walk into a police station and deliver gratuities to some lieutenant without a moment of suspicion falling upon him. He could look after Inez, whenever she had one of her tantrums. That's how he first wended his way to the Ansonia. He would buy her a little gift out of his own pocket—a trinket, or a paper flower, and she wore that flower in her hair. Even while his heart beat like a mad drum, he wasn't disloyal to AR. But Inez's perfume did intoxicate the boy.

And when she got too crazy in her loneliness, he would warn AR.

"Arnold, you might consider making a trip to the Ansonia. Otherwise you'll have open warfare. And I can't predict the consequences."

"Little man, are you my brain, or not? Bring her here."

And that's what David loved the most—when he squired Inez into the delicatessen. The usual hubbub died at the first sight of her. She was regal with her long legs. That's what David thought. She couldn't have broken every man's heart had she not been a dancer. And there were very few women at Lindy's—except for showgirls, like Inez.

How could he ever describe her walk? She wouldn't wiggle her derriere. It was like the stroll of a delicious panther. She'd found a particular shape for her wildness, even when she screamed at AR. And she either screamed or purred at him, in front of the whole delicatessen. And Arnold didn't shiver, didn't react. He sat with his sad eyes until Inez started to laugh. Because she couldn't stay angry at him.

David loved the nights when Inez was there. She'd sit without her shoes, twist one toe around his ankle, not to provoke him, but to reveal her bond with David. He was the little king next to the king and his paramour, his second *wife*. No one could get to AR without a nod from David. He could open or close a deal while he whispered into Arnold's ear. But the boy couldn't partake in the delicatessen's full electrical storm. AR sent him home before midnight.

"I can't risk losing you, kid. You might turn into a pumpkin."

By this time, David was managing all of Arnold's accounts. He pocketed nothing for himself, but he still had access to Arnold's money. He signed Arnold's markers, and David's signature was good as gold. He took all the blame for Arnold's death. It had nothing to do with that midnight curfew. He had to run an errand for his dad, and by the time he got to Lindy's, Arnold had met his own fate at the Park Central. David would never have allowed him to keep that rendezvous with a shill from the bankers who wanted his blood.

The boy didn't panic. He sat at Arnold's table, even after the funeral. He revealed none of his grief. He had most of Arnold's gunsels behind him. Markers were called in. Debts were paid. He had the capital to keep Inez at the Ansonia. He was loyal to her until the day she died. But David's rise was unprecedented in Manhattan's own mythology of crime. He ruled the Rothstein mob at fifteen, though it wasn't a real mob, just a ragtag collection of button men. Arnold had liked it this way. Nothing could ever be blamed on him.

David had to quit high school. He had no time for books. He moved into the Ansonia before he was sixteen. He was much too young to sign a lease, but the Ansonia let him in. And God forgive him, but he was disloyal to Arnold's ghost. He made love to Inez. He could waft her perfume from a mile away. He slept inside her armpit, and he wanted no other goddess. Now her tantrums fell on him. He adored every moment.

"Davey," she'd coo, "didn't Arnold's little man promise to take me to France?"

"Inez, if I left town for five minutes, I'd be dead."

"You never even go to Lindy's anymore. You sit in this damn tomb."

"But I'm alive as long as I sit."

Both of them couldn't stop mourning AR. And he wouldn't allow her to change one picture in her apartment. They were accomplices when they made love, in spite of their passion. He was devoted to her. When she grew ill, he took care of Inez, sat with her, read to her from one of the books he loved. He'd always been a reader. That was his one diversion, his one device, other than gambling. He'd gamble his shirt away and get it back, while he read to her about a woman named Emma Bovary who was devoured by the silliness of her own desire. . . .

They saw themselves in Emma, who might have survived had she ever had her own AR. And even with all his wiles, and his kisses, he couldn't console Inez. She grew weaker and weaker. He offered to take her to France, wearing his velvet slippers, since he never wore shoes anymore. But it was too late. Inez seemed ravaged with remorse. She slipped away, died in her sleep.

None of his associates could bring this prince of the Ansonia out of his melancholy. He sat in his lair, buying up more and more of Manhattan. No one knew how rich he was, not even David. He had his own private bank; he was its first and last customer and client. He prospered through recessions, through bull and bear markets. He missed Inez, wouldn't rent out her apartment on the thirteenth floor. Wandering through that apartment in his slippers was David's only solace.

The years passed. He never invited call girls up to his lair. He wasn't looking for some replica of Inez. There was no such girl. His teeth began to crumble. David didn't care. And then his manager told him about a bimbo who couldn't pay her rent. Trudy Winckleman, lately of New Orleans. She had no claims on the apartment. Some "gentleman" had paid for her upkeep. But there were complications. The bimbo had two kids—and the city didn't like throwing single mothers out onto the street, not while the Big Guy was mayor.

David had her brought up to his labyrinth without her two brats. He meant to give her a check, sign her right out of the building, so that she would no longer be a nuisance.

And then he saw the bimbo with her silver hair. She didn't grovel; she didn't beg. His hand shivered as he scratched out the sums and figures on the check. He couldn't believe it. The bimbo had Inez's own insolence, the same pinched smile that could eat your heart out. She was no replica, no rehearsed reincarnation. She was just *another* Inez, even if her legs weren't so long and she wasn't blessed with Inez's blondness. He didn't stall. He made her a proposition.

She smiled. "And I suppose I'll have to warm up your old bones. King David and his Abishag."

"Girlie," he said like a gunsel, "I could have you killed. . . . You'd never leave this floor. They'd stuff you right into the attic."

"Good," she said. "Then I wouldn't have to leave the Ansonia."

She'd dismantled whatever power he had over her. He had to beg her to stay, but he still was stubborn: she'd have to live in Inez's apartment and promise not to change a stick of furniture.

"That's marvelous," she said. "A bordello at the Ansonia. How many of your business partners will I have to sleep with?"

"David Pearl isn't a pimp," he said. "But you can't live there with your kids. They might jump around and ruin all the relics."

Now he used all his sway. He had her brats installed at the best private school in Connecticut. She could visit them as often as she liked, but they couldn't come to the Ansonia. And she was the one who began calling herself Inez.

"King David, I'm living in a mausoleum. I might as well be one of its members."

She'd solved the riddle of his loneliness. He'd come downstairs in the middle of the night, lie down next to her, and she'd hold him in her arms, as if he were made of glass—Inez's little glass man. He'd moan softly as she rubbed his forehead. He dozed for five minutes; David lived without sleep. And then he'd return to his lair.

She began doing favors for him, was soon his "social secretary." She entertained the rare visitors that David had, sat with them, served wine. But no one dared touch Inez. And then he started to panic. The Big Guy was too embroiled in the Bronx. And David maneuvered to kick him upstairs, to have him sink into the darkness of a vice president's domain. But Sidel was a stubborn son of a bitch. David had to find a secret weapon. His little protégé had been enthralled with tales of Rothstein and Inez. So David lured him into the Ansonia, let him feast upon his social secretary.

And now he had to undo all of Isaac's damage. He had to take drastic measures—leave his lair at the Ansonia for a whole afternoon and meet with the Texas barons, nabobs and military men who couldn't be seen at the Ansonia and were his secret partners in Sidereal. The barons had arrived from Houston, Dallas, and San Antone and descended upon a motel in New Jersey, with all their bodyguards from some remote enclave within military intelligence. They were all in mufti, even the generals, and had blocked off an entire wing of the motel, which looked out upon a modern-day castle where medieval jousts were held.

The generals had sent their own driver in a sleek sedan. David still wore his slippers and the same corroded sweater with patches on the sleeves, while Inez was dressed to kill. She stepped into the sedan in a skin-tight sheath and silver sandals. David groaned while they sat under the blinking lights of the Lincoln Tunnel. Inez had to hold his hand once they crossed the Jersey flatlands. The stench was unbearable to David, who was giddy by the time they got to the motel.

The bodyguards were in awe of him and had been told not to stare at his slippers. But they couldn't keep their eyes off Inez. "The maestro has landed," they whispered into their button mikes. They had to frisk Inez. They used one of their battery-charged machines, and the perfume from her armpits made them delirious. She could have shot out their eyes.

"I'm hungry," David muttered. The motel was attached to a delicatessen, and that's where David met the barons. But it wasn't Lindy's, even though this dump advertised itself as a "Lindy's-style delicatessen." It irked David. Lindy's meant nothing without AR. It had become one more logo, one more brand name with mediocre pastrami.

They had a corner table, far from this delicatessen's usual traffic. The bodyguards had scanned the area for hidden microphones. They weren't worried about the Secret Service or Bull Latham's Bureau. They had to be careful of their own competitors, industrial spies from Houston.

They didn't introduce themselves. They had code names: Mr. Dallas, Mr. Houston, Mr. Abilene. . . . David was Mr. Manhattan, and Inez, whom they had never met, was Mrs. Cassandra. They had a complete dossier on her, but they didn't trust their own files. She could have been a plant from some super-secret agency. But none of them had realized how beautiful she was. Among themselves, they called her the Sorcerer's Apprentice.

David wouldn't touch the pastrami. He had a side order of half-sour pickles. He demanded a glass of milk and a chocolate chip cookie. That was Rothstein's favorite snack. Milk and cookies.

"Gentlemen," he said. "You have your warriors, I have mine. I don't want Sidel touched."

"Mr. Manhattan, he's hampering us. He won't go away. And we're betting that the president-elect will crash. Isaac is the real contender."

"Contend, contend," David said. "Once he leaves the mayor's office, he's harmless. He'll have less teeth in his mouth than I have."

"We can't take a chance," said Mr. Abilene, who was worth half a billion and had a scar under his mouth.

"Then I walk away from this deal," David said. "And you'll have bubkes in the Bronx."

"Don't get so hairy," said Mr. Houston, an oil magnate who was a graduate of Rice. "You want to leave this table with your own two feet, don't you, son?"

David began to cackle. "Kiddos, I had a similar thought. Look around you. Every fucking customer in this little cafeteria belongs to me. You can call yourselves my prisoners."

"He's bluffing," said Mr. Abilene, a general at Brooks Air Force Base. "Let's show Mr. Manhattan our firepower."

"I wouldn't," said Inez, with a neutral smile. "Just ask for our waitress."

The waitress appeared. She looked like an aging flower child.

"Miss Inez, should I tell these big bad men what they can expect if they don't behave?"

"Yes, darling."

"There's a little tub of plastique molded right into the table. It's enough to blow up half of New Jersey. . . . Can I take your orders, gentlemen?"

The barons had lost their appetite. They spread out a map of the Bronx across the table. Mr. Abilene was their spokesman.

"Sir, can you promise us an unrestricted path from Webster Avenue downward, across Tremont and Morrisania, including Crotona Park? Of course, the streets themselves will disappear."

"And the housing projects?" asked Mr. San Antone.

"We'll relocate the projects," said David. "We won't leave a living soul without a much better apartment, on the far side of the Bronx River."

"And it's a question of public relations. We can't steal land from the living or the dead. And we can't push the city around. Our pitch is that we're revitalizing the Bronx; we're creating a community. We'll lease the whole shebang and convert it into federal land. We can't put up a teepee without that conversion. New York will have a windfall—its own military base a mile from Manhattan. We'll put up hundreds of housing units. We'll grow new wetlands. We'll build a river right into the rocks. But we won't have a bunch of local Commies picketing us. It'll look bad for the United States."

"You'll be the white knights of Texas," David said, "saviors of a dying borough."

"Not all white," said Mr. Abilene. "We'll need a black general or two on our board . . . and a Native American, if we can find one."

"It's good for the Reservation," said Mr. Dallas. That was the code name for their future Bronx base: the Reservation. "And there aren't any holdouts in your portfolio, are there, Mr. Manhattan? We wouldn't want any sudden surprises . . . picking up land that doesn't belong to us."

"It's ninety percent in my pocket," David said.

"And the other ten? We can't move in without acquiring all the leases. The Prez is dying to make an announcement. It would be a real feather in the poor fucker's hat. Calder Cottonwood, champion of the Bronx."

"Mr. Dallas," David said, "you can tell Cottonwood that he'll have his last stand in the Bronx's own Indian country—or I'll tell him himself."

"And if Sidel interferes, if he gets in the way?"

David didn't stumble. "Then I'll dispose of him myself."

He got up from the table with Inez and never looked once at his silent partners.

"Should I call your driver?" asked Mr. Abilene.

"No," David said. "I have my own man . . . and should you decide to follow us, I'd look around you first."

The delicatessen was deserted—it was as if locusts had descended upon the new Lindy's and wiped it clean. There wasn't a loaf of bread or a pickle jar to be found. The waiters and waitresses were all gone. There wasn't a single customer.

"I wouldn't move for half an hour," David said. "The plastique is a bit temperamental. Sometimes it has a mind of its own."

And he rushed out in his slippers, Inez right beside him.

■ ■ ■

THE INEZ CORPORATION OWNED MANHATTAN'S biggest limousine service, and David had a hundred drivers at his disposal. But he didn't want a limo. It would have been much too easy to derail. Who could trust these madmen from the Alamo? They were all kissing cousins from another planet. But he had to lease the land to them. No one else was big enough to buy up "the whole shebang," as Mr. San Antone had said. David had fond memories of San Antonio. He'd accompanied AR to the Menger Hotel in '25, before there was a River Walk, and that bend in the San Antonio River was little more than a downtown sewer. AR had gone there to gamble. David fell in love with the gold spittoons. He was AR's portable bank, with cash in every pocket. That lunatic lost three hundred grand in less than an hour. He didn't have three hundred grand. David had to sign all the markers. . . .

He'd rented an armored bus. It stood outside the delicatessen. He climbed aboard with Inez. He had a couple of shooters, but that was just for show. If the Texas barons wrecked his bus in the middle of New Jersey, it would have created much too big a stink. They would have to kiss their Bronx Reservation good-bye and look for some painted desert in the badlands of South Dakota. David was still valuable to the barons, but for how long?

He began to shiver on board the bus. Inez had to rock him in her arms. He couldn't have maneuvered the barons without Inez. Her appearance at his side had stunned them. They could deal with their relic of a partner in his velvet slippers, but not with Inez.

He was still shivering when he arrived at the Ansonia. Inez brought him upstairs to her own apartment. She undressed him, as if he were a fanciful child with white hair, and she ran a bath for David, helped him sit down in the light-blue porcelain tub that AR had installed for his blond mistress. But this Inez wasn't even ashamed to soap David's balls.

"Sweetheart," he said. "I'll surprise you one afternoon, and I'll rape you to pieces."

She laughed, but it wasn't unkind. And he thought of Sidel. That miserable man didn't have much of a future. Someone would have to fix his wagon.

14

THEY WERE BACK AGAIN, THOSE army engineers. This time they camped in Crotona Park, which was much more desolate than that other park on a hill. There was talk that the wild dogs of Crotona Park had once been as tame as pussycats. They had belonged to the drug lords of Tremont and Morrisania, and their wives and children. Wars and police raids had scattered the gangs, and now their dogs roamed the badlands, rooting with their noses right into baby carriages. But they weren't clever enough for the army engineers, who left dolls in baby carriages on the shores of Indian Lake; the dogs were decimated with the arms and legs of dolls in their mouths. . . .

Isaac mourned Indian Lake; it had once been the preferred vacation ground of poor Italians and Jews near the park. There was nothing like it in the midst of the mating season, when young gallants with gold wristbands fluttered around the prettiest girls of Crotona Park, who paraded in summer midriffs that revealed a single band of flesh. Isaac wished he had been one of those gallants. But he was already a cop. And Robert Moses' tunnel in the sky would ruin that mating season, as it passed right over the northern edge of the park in the late 1950s. Perhaps it would have been ruined without Robert Moses. But at least the Bronx wouldn't have had a concrete ribbon across its spine.

And it might not have had an epidemic of army engineers. But Isaac couldn't seem to catch them in their tracks. They would appear in one location, then move into some mirror or mirage. The Bronx itself had become an enormous mirror, and was as much of a mirage as David Pearl's limestone castle. But Isaac couldn't master mirages. So he sat down with his property clerk, his finance chiefs, and other mavens before the army engineers could finish mapping the badlands. Isaac went through the city's books, block by block. He closed his eyes, and his finger landed on Bryant Avenue in Morrisania, which contained a whole mountain of rubble. His commissioners called it East Berlin.

"That's where we'll build it," Isaac said.

"Build what?" said one of the mavens. "Mr. Mayor, what are you talking about?"

"A junior high school—for ghetto geniuses. It will rise right out of the rubble as the new home of the Merliners—Marianna will attend the school."

"But she'll be in the White House," said his maven from the Board of Ed.

"Means nothing," Isaac mumbled. "Marianna can commute from Pennsylvania Avenue. And we'll also build a shelter for the homeless."

"Boss," said his own executive assistant, "you can't do diddle without the City Planning Commission."

"Well, don't I sit on that commission?"

His mavens looked at him as if he were the mayor of another planet. "Not a chance, sir. And even if you did, they'd run you out of their rooms at Spector Hall. You're something of a lame duck."

"Where's Spector Hall?" he groaned. The city itself was a labyrinth beyond the mayor's control. He had no idea who worked for him and who didn't. He had more commissioners than Alexander the Great.

He dismissed all his mavens and called in his press secretary. He'd have to plot a media campaign, plant an interview here and there. He could have met with the *New York Times*. The *Times* had called him the best mayor the city had ever had, after Fiorello La Guardia, the Little Flower. La Guardia had raced to fires in a fire chief's helmet, had tossed slot machines into the Hudson, had been the guest conductor of the city's own orchestra, had read the funny papers to children over the radio, and Isaac was only a thug with a gun. He couldn't compete with the Little Flower. Also, the *Times* was considered a Commie rag in Texas. Isaac would have to connect with the *Wall Street Journal*.

The *Journal* was one of the few dailies in the land that had supported Calder Cottonwood. It despised Isaac Sidel and called Michael a crook. And it wasn't so wrong when it claimed that Isaac had ties with the Mob. Jesus, how else could you preside over a labyrinth? The Maf could catch a child molester, settle a strike between the city and its cantankerous unions. Isaac would have disappeared inside a shitstorm without the Mob.

He invited Raphael Roberts, his severest critic on the *Journal*, to the vice president–elect's suite at the Ansonia. Raphael was a gnome of a man who'd been excoriating Isaac ever since his days as police commissioner. He wore a rumpled suit; his shoes were as battered as the mayor's. And Isaac had to wonder what kind of picture this unpolished gnome presented in the offices of the *Journal*.

Raphael ranted from the moment he arrived at Isaac's headquarters. But he was astonished that the vice president–elect didn't have one assistant, one extra desk.

"I'm not sympathetic to anything you've done, Mr. Mayor, or anything you'll ever do. And I doubt that the *Journal* would take kindly to one of your so-called scoops."

"Jesus," Isaac said, "will ya listen before you bite my head off? I'm not that different from the Prez. He wants to rebuild the inner cities. Hasn't he swooped down over the Bronx in his eagle?"

"What eagle?" asked the columnist.

"*Marine One.* He wants to resurrect the bombed-out streets, and so do I."

Reluctantly, Raphael began to scratch a few words in his notebook. "And what's your program, Mr. Mayor?"

"Satellites," Isaac said. "I'll build a junior high school for my Merliners and a shelter for the homeless . . . and a golden age club right in the middle of those mean streets. I'll have satellites everywhere, and surround them with new neighborhoods."

"And how will you acquire all that property?"

"Through the right of eminent domain."

Raphael continued to scratch with his pen. "But won't that cripple small-property owners? You might have to tear down the corner candy store."

"Raphael, wake up. There are no corner candy stores in that heart of darkness. They were swept away with all the fires. And Moses couldn't have built his highway without eminent domain. He ripped through entire neighborhoods near Tremont, left a fucking desert."

"Ah," Raphael said. "You're not going to suck me into that old argument. The South Bronx would have died with or without Robert Moses. And it would have fallen off the map long ago without Yankee Stadium. And don't think I'm going to praise that prick Michael for bullying the owners into submission. I would have preferred a long baseball strike. Without a salary cap, you'll turn every pint-sized slugger into a multimillionaire."

"I didn't bring you here to talk baseball," the Big Guy groaned.

"Then why did you bring me?"

And for a moment Isaac thought that Raphael himself might be part of the Texas Mafia.

"Why?" Isaac said. "To give you and the *Journal* a chance to crucify Isaac Sidel . . . I'm going to make Moses look like a pygmy and a piker. I'll tear down his highway if I have to. I'm going to build and build in all the debris."

Raphael had stopped scribbling. "Mr. Mayor, you're going to leave office in little more than a month. What can you hope to accomplish?"

"As much as I can."

Raphael Roberts left without shaking Isaac's hand. But the Big Guy was ebullient. He was convinced the *Journal* would lacerate him by the end of the week. He could already imagine Raphael's column: *The Great Dictator's Last Mad Days in Manhattan*.

But he didn't even have much time to gloat. He could sense someone outside his door. Had another silly assassin come to shoot out his lights? Isaac was getting sick of these staged affairs. He opened the door while his Glock fell through the waistband of his pants and bounced off his left loafer. He didn't even bother to pick it up. And there she was in her silver helmet, as substantial as a wraith.

"Isaac," she whispered, "that isn't nice. It's bad luck to leave a lady standing in a door."

And he swept her inside with all his bearish charm. It could have been part of some primitive mating season. His tongue was inside her face while they danced across Isaac's own political parlor. He hadn't slept here once, preferring to ride uptown to Gracie Mansion after midnight. It had nothing to do with the comforts of a mayor's bed. He was still in mourning without the Little First Lady, who'd been his houseguest until Tim Seligman and the DNC stole her from him. But he liked to wake up and find a breakfast tray outside his door. The mayor's bedroom was a fortress, under a keyless lock. No one could enter without the combination.

There'd always be a flower with his pot of coffee and his morning mail. And if he was lucky enough, his chauffeur might have driven to Sutton Place South and returned with a batch of butternut cookies from Marianna Storm. And here he was without a mattress in his own Bedouin encampment at the Ansonia. But the Big Guy didn't need a mattress. He lay with Inez on the Ansonia's hardwood herringbone floor. For all his anger and deep distrust, he was tender with her.

Isaac couldn't help himself. He was forever falling in love with some faithless creature. And why should this false Inez be any different? But perhaps his emotion was all twisted up with AR and that first Inez. He didn't need Einstein or Freud to tell him that the simplest of suitors was most often a voyeur. He was like a baby who'd ravished his very own ravisher.

What more could Isaac say? He was in love with Trudy Winckleman of New Orleans, a.k.a. Inez.

"It's David who sent you here, isn't it? There is no Cassandra's Wall. David hired some starving actors to play billionaires. And you're the biggest actress of them all."

"But that's what turns you on," she said.

Isaac wasn't much of a grand inquisitor. Even a false Inez had to have her own AR. But they kissed with a hunger that couldn't have been rehearsed. Isaac's mouth was swollen after five minutes. His sudden delight took him out of that land of woe he seemed to live in. Her aromas made him delirious.

"Live with me," Isaac muttered.

She laughed. "Shall I become the official mistress of Gracie Mansion?"

"No," he said. "Move out of that mausoleum on the thirteenth floor. We'll go someplace—hide. I don't care."

"Darling," she said. "I can't run. It's a little too late. But you should get out of the Ansonia. It will give you a lot of grief."

"Ah," Isaac said. "It's my sacred font. I grew up with the Ansonia in my blood. And without the Ansonia, I wouldn't have met you."

"Darling, I'm David's employee."

"You're a miracle," he said.

She laughed again. "But some miracles are good, and some are bad. You've been like a son to David, but he'll have to kill you in the end. Maybe it's a sign of respect. He's a very troubled executioner. But I won't stop him, Isaac. Each hour you survive, you get more and more in his way. The next time I visit you . . . "

"It will be with a dagger in your hand."

"Then don't open your door to strangers," she said.

"But you aren't a stranger."

"Oh, yes, I am."

She gathered her articles of clothing, and she was gone, dancing out his door half-undressed, her thighs like magnificent, supple sticks. It took him less than a minute to mourn her absence. He still had his Mafia "gonnegtions." He could have kidnapped Inez. But what a price he'd have to pay. And he wasn't worried about the wizard's wrath. He was worried about Inez. She would have mocked Isaac without a moment of mercy in her eyes. And that he couldn't have borne.

■ ■ ■

IT WAS HER BABIES, HER babies. She'd brought them with her from New Orleans. *Daniel and Darl.* She didn't want to ruin them in the ruins of her own life. Her babies were almost as tall as she. They'd grown up in a bordello. And they had the wild-eyed habits of whores, though Daniel was very shy. She was cultivating them at a private school in Connecticut, where they had to wear uniforms and pledge allegiance to their school song. Daniel would be fine, protected by an older sister who would claw out the eyes of anyone who wanted to harm him. But who would protect Darl? She stood out at school, a twelve-year-old woman among children of the privileged class—no uniform could hide the contours of her body.

It tore at Inez's heart to see her there, the lone female in an infants' world, hungry for something else. Inez fought with her every time she visited that damn school. Daniel would start to bawl and hide behind his sister's shoulder.

"Mommy, Mommy, go away."

And Darl would smile at her like the whore of Babylon . . . or Basin Street. God, she'd picked up every habit—she was as mean as a walking hurricane.

"Mother, how nice of you to visit."

"Don't get sassy," she said.

Darl's eyes were the color of honey. She could have sashayed out of the schoolyard, gone to the nearest bank, and gotten a job. She was twelve . . . and looked twenty-five. Inez didn't want any of the teachers or custodians at this school to handle Darl. She'd told that to David Pearl. *I'll kill them myself,* she'd said. And David had put the fear of God into the trustees at Walden Pond School. He was the school's biggest benefactor. Walden Pond was where David sent children he or one of his associates had to hide. But Inez didn't trust that old man, and she didn't trust Darl. She could see the trace of lipstick on her daughter's mouth.

"Darl, if you misbehave . . . "

Darl's eyes turned the color of smoke. Then that smoke disappeared and she started to imitate her own mother, with one hand on her hip. And the three of them laughed and cried. Daniel had crept out from behind his sister's shoulder. He hugged Inez and Darl with all his heart.

"Stay with us, Mommy, stay."

And it no longer mattered to Inez what she had to do. She'd lead Sidel by the nose, play Mata Hari for the rest of her life, as long as her babies were snug in their uniforms. She'd make love to the devil himself if it would guarantee that Darl could keep her cherry for another five years. But Isaac wasn't the devil. He was Inez's own strange troubadour. And a girl like her from New Orleans was a sucker for troubadours.

15

T WAS AN ELABORATE GAME of hide-and-seek, romance in the middle of a war maneuver. She'd run from him and he'd find her. Or she would find him. Isaac didn't care how prominent he'd become. He would have loved to squire his dark lady of New Orleans around town. But she was frightened of losing her children. If her picture appeared in all the papers with or without Isaac, her past might pop out, and some government agency would call her an unfit mother. So the dark lady met Isaac in the dark. They'd tiptoe into a movie house after the feature started, or find a whacked-out Cantonese restaurant at the border of Chinatown where Isaac Sidel was just another name. He was *almost* content in his delirium over Inez. He would drink in the musk of her body, fondle her knee while they had tofu and spinach with garlic sauce.

But they had no real venue of their own. She couldn't spend the night with him at his mansion, no matter how secretive he was—they would have woken to the noise of reporters on the lawn. He couldn't stay with her in that mausoleum on the thirteenth floor. It would have been like undressing in front of David Pearl and Arnold Rothstein's ghost. So they camped out at Isaac's headquarters. And no matter what their passion, and their hunger to touch, she'd wake up in the middle of the night and return to her mausoleum.

His dark lady began to develop deep furrows in her brow. She'd pour sugar into her wine at the Cantonese restaurant. "Isaac, I can't sneak around. That old man will steal my babies. I'll never see them again."

"I'll steal them back."

The furrows deepened. "Stay out of this, darling, you have to leave me alone."

"And if I can't."

"Then both of us will suffer."

"But we could run away with your kids. I don't care. The Democrats can find another vice president."

"Shut up," she said. "I'm running away every time I'm with you. . . . Don't you dare follow me, Isaac, or I'll scratch your eyes out."

"Scratch," he said. "You might pity a blind man."

She got up from the table in that ruinous restaurant, had her last gulp of sugared wine, and said, "I'm the one you ought to pity."

She ran from him again. He found a note under his door when he returned to the Ansonia.

I love you. Leave me alone.

That plea broke the Big Guy's heart. He stopped pursuing her. His life had become one long mirror and mirage. He loved her kids without ever having met them. He didn't even know their names. She'd never shown him a picture of her "babies."

He was forlorn without Inez. But at least the *Wall Street Journal* hadn't disappointed Sidel. It talked about his flagrant land grabs, said the mayor was acting like an African potentate, and that if he wasn't stopped, half the Bronx would fall under eminent domain. It was the usual sound and fury. Isaac would have had to plead with a hundred boards and commissions, sit with the city's own chief counsel, to even contemplate building one junior high in the heart of darkness. But the damage was done. Raphael Robert's column in the *Journal* gave the illusion that Isaac and his city planners had already moved into the Bronx and were seizing enormous tracts of land.

And Isaac decided to disappear for a little while. He was retracing his steps. He would commune with Billy Bob Archer, learn more about the eye of God. He had an itch to see that first shooter, even if he had to break into the mental ward at Fort Sam. But it wasn't so easy. He couldn't ask the DNC to charter a plane, and if he had to fly to San Antone, the Secret Service would have to go over the logistics of his journey. There'd have to be a sky marshal aboard the trip to Dallas and the connecting flight, and he would bring havoc to any airline that accommodated him.

It took three whole days, and when he arrived at JFK, half the airport was blocked. He was rambling around, signing autographs, with Martin Boyle a few feet away, when he was grabbed under the shoulder and whisked in another direction. In five minutes he couldn't be found. He was wearing a fake nose. *Jesus, are they gonna whack me right in the terminal?*

He wasn't even scared . . . until he recognized the white glove of his son-in-law, Joe Barbarossa. Joey's hand had been burned in Saigon, and that hand never really healed. So he had to wear the white glove. He was the most decorated cop in Manhattan, and he'd also been the biggest drug dealer in Nam. He'd freelanced a lot until he fell in love with Marilyn, Isaac's wild-eyed only daughter. Isaac didn't want Marilyn to marry that lunatic, who'd become his own adjutant. Vietnam Joe was invaluable. The whole of Manhattan and half the Bronx were frightened of him. He knew all the dealers, most of whom had been his partners in Nam. And he knew all the assassins.

"Jesus, Joey, why the fuck are you following me? You ought to be home with Marilyn."

He'd avoided Marilyn and Joe during the campaign, wouldn't pose with them, because he didn't want his daughter to become the easy target of some insane assassin, like Billy Bob. Yet here was Joey in the flesh. . . .

"Are you listening? Martin Boyle will put you in a cage? I'm going to Dallas."

"There's been a change of plans," said Joe Barbarossa, who was a much bigger bandit than Legs Diamond or any of AR's other button boys. Most of the cops who'd worked for Isaac were heavy hitters. He drew madmen and freaks into the undercurrent of his own mad wake.

"We're going to Houston," his son-in-law said.

"But Houston's not on my itinerary. You'll have to tell Martin Boyle."

"Dad," Joe said, grinding his teeth like a wolf. "Boyle's part of the problem."

"What are you saying? He's sworn to protect me."

"But he hasn't sworn enough."

"I'll kill you," Isaac said. "He's my favorite Secret Service man. And how do I know that someone hasn't hired you to put out my lights?"

"That's the problem, Dad. Someone has hired me . . . or else I wouldn't be here."

■ ■ ■

HE WAS GLUM ON THE flight. No one recognized him with that fake schnozzola he had to wear. He began to brood as his son-in-law told him a very tall tale about Saigon. Half the *ville* was dealing drugs, he said. The war was winding down. "Dad, it was fucking surreal." Saigon wasn't much safer than Indian country. It was called El Paso East. "And Cholon, where all the chinks and the deserters lived, with the other crazies, was called Tijuana West."

"Joey, Joey," Isaac said, nursing a glass of milk and an airline cookie, "what does this have to do with Billy Bob Archer and Martin Boyle."

"Hold your horses," his son-in-law said.

Joey dealt drugs right out of the American embassy. It was a madhouse in 1974. The war had never been winnable, according to

Joe. Charlie was the only one who had a real stake in Nam—but the Americans had Saigon and had turned it into West Texas. The half-breed whores spoke with an El Paso drawl. Enchiladas were sold on every corner, along with Corona beer.

"Joey, get to the point?"

"We needed protection."

The drug dealers had their own crazy wars, which were an outgrowth of the war itself, where corporals shot their own sergeants, and every officer was fair game for some grunt who didn't like the color of his captain's eyes. There was complete chaos in '74. Kissinger was talking peace behind the generals' backs. And everybody wanted to rip off Vietnam Joe. He had to hire the Crusaders. They'd been a special unit inside military intel. They turned invisible once they hit Indian country. "They could tear the fucking heart out of a Vietcong village."

"Joey, you mean they were assassins who improvised."

"Something like that. And I hired those scary mothers to protect my ass. They cut off fingers, took scalps. And I never lost an ounce of my shit. . . . Dad, what was the name of that colonel at the military madhouse in San Antone?"

"I can't recall."

"A colonel with white, white hair and eyes as pale as Mr. Death."

"Trevor Welles," Isaac groaned.

"He was the Crusaders' main man. There was nothing to do anymore, no tribal chieftains to kill, none of Charlie's tunnels to smoke out, so they hired themselves out to the highest bidders. I paid them in dope and huge bricks of cash . . . but I never realized they had gone domestic, not until yesterday. I thought they had disbanded years ago. And that makes me suspicious. I think they're freelancing for some mavericks inside the Pentagon. It's El Paso West all over again."

"How do ya know?"

"That crazy colonel called me on the phone, asked me to smoke you . . . said the Ansonia billionaire would pay me more scratch than I had ever seen."

"But he's not stupid. He knows you're my son-in-law."

"That's the whole point, Dad. The colonel is sending me a kite. I play along with him, say you're all zippered up with Secret Service men, that Martin Boyle is practically your son. You drink Dr Pepper out of the same tin can."

The Big Guy had begun to shake. He didn't want to hear the rest . . . and had to hear it.

"And what did that devil say?"

"Dad, I swear to God. The colonel says that Martin Boyle wasn't such a good son in San Antone, or they never could have gotten to you."

"But it doesn't make sense," Isaac said. "Dennis Cohen had to be tied to the same conspiracy, and he wanted to whack Martin Boyle in the Ansonia's attic."

But it no longer mattered what Isaac said in this madcap game of chess. Joey had the black *and* white queens in his pocket, and he hit Isaac with both queens at once.

"Boyle had second thoughts. That's what I figure. And Mr. Ansonia tried to get rid of him. But none of them considered your Glock."

"And now Mr. Ansonia wants to get rid of me."

"He's been trying, Dad. But that little mother can't make up his mind. He's like that other fucking assassin."

Isaac grew as dizzy as little Alice hurtling down the rabbit hole. Everywhere he went was a new mirror and mirage.

"For God's sake, Joey. What assassin?"

"You know, Dad. He's in a book—a prince who leaves a trail of corpses. His sweetheart drowns herself because of him, his own little mama gets poisoned, and he stabs his stepfather in the heart on account of hearsay from a ghost."

"Hamlet," Isaac muttered.

"That's the guy. Hamlet is living in the Ansonia right now. And he still can't make up his mind about you."

"Then why are we going to Houston?"

"To meet with Mr. Death."

16

H E PLUCKED OFF HIS FALSE nose once he got to the Warwick and registered as Isaac Sidel. This dinosaur of a hotel had once been the watering hole of rich cattlemen, when they rode off the plains and could watch boys wrestle with the crocodiles in the bayous. Isaac had never seen a crocodile in Houston, but the cockroaches were as big as a man's finger and the flies as fat as a strawberry. From his windows on the seventh floor, he could survey the ribbed streets and brown grassland of Rice University, and the various beltways that looked like the bluish veins on Isaac's own arm.

"Jesus," Isaac said, "couldn't we go to the Galleria? I want to have some fun."

"Dad, Dad, your life's in danger. We have to wait for Trevor Welles."

They ordered a light dinner. But Isaac couldn't eat his lamb chop. He had some crackers and goat cheese, drank a glass of Medoc. And Trevor Welles arrived without a knock on the door. He wasn't dressed as a colonel this time. He wore a sweat suit, like some harebrained college coach. But he had the same startling white hair. Even in his clownish costume, he was Mr. Death.

They all sat on a sofa near the Warwick's picture windows, with Houston's beltways below them, those bluish arteries jumping across the plains. Isaac could have been looking down onto a futuristic Bronx, with all the badlands swept away.

"I apologize, Mr. President," said Trevor Welles. "But there was a rotten turn of events. And we never realized how close you were to your son-in-law. We had bad intel."

"That's grand," Isaac said. "Now tell me what the fuck is going on before I strangle both of you."

"Sir, you might catch me. But not Vietnam Joe. The gooks shit a brick whenever Joe was in Indian country."

"I thought he never left Saigon," Isaac said.

"Unless he was with the Crusaders. He had more kills than my very best man."

Isaac began to sulk in front of the two assassins. "Then you lied to me, Joey. It was like a cover story. Barbarossa of Saigon, who dealt dope next door to the American ambassador. . . . I trusted you, let you have Marilyn."

"But lying saved your life, sir. If he hadn't married your daughter, you wouldn't be here."

Isaac was still in that rabbit hole, more confused then ever. But he was drawn to the crazed chivalry of assassins.

"Who hired you, Mr. Welles?"

"Ah," said Trevor, "that's a complicated tale. In the long run, I work for Calder Cottonwood. The presidency has impoverished him. But when he returns to Texas, he'll be one of the richest men on the planet."

"Are you telling me that he wanted to lose the election?"

"*Want*, sir, is too weak a word. But he was still playing the percentages. It's called Texas poker. There's no united front among the bankers and oilmen. A good number of them gave millions to Mr. Storm's campaign. They despise the president-elect, but they'd sell one of their own kidneys for you."

Now the Big Guy was really groaning. "Then all they wanted was a shitstorm."

"That's right. They were betting on a constitutional crisis. But they misjudged you, sir. They thought they could get you to lie down. But you're like a West Texas badman. The more people you kill, the more you're loved."

"Come on," Isaac said, "you're talking with cotton candy in your mouth. Who hired you to hit me inside the cattleman's bar?"

"Mr. David Pearl. Oh, he didn't want you dead, just permanently disabled. But his own fat bitch got in the way, little Amanda. We would have finished the story, and then Joey stepped into the frame. We can't afford to have him on our blind side."

"What happens now?" Isaac had to ask. He'd drawn another madman into the fold.

"The Crusaders will protect your life for three weeks . . . until the Electoral College votes and Congress certifies that vote in January. Then we're done. Both you and Mr. Storm can piss in the bucket after that. But until then, God knows who will be gunning for you."

"And what about that fucking fort in the Bronx, with David Pearl leasing land to the Pentagon?"

"Mr. President, I can't protect you on every front."

"Stop it," Isaac said. "What kind of commission will you get if that fort is built?"

"More than you'll ever make if you lived in the White House for a hundred years."

Isaac got up from the sofa and began to pace across his grandiose sitting room at the Warwick.

"Dad, Dad," Joey said, "will ya listen to Trev? The clock is ticking while we talk."

"All right, what do I have to do?"

"Stay in Texas. You'll go out on the road again. We'll ask the Dems for their yellow bus. We'll avoid the big cities."

"And what do I tell the American people?"

"That the vice president–elect is on a special mission to introduce himself to the real America—not the bankers, not the fat cats, but the hardscrabble farmers, the fishermen along the bayous, the dirt poor . . . "

"In the woods and the wetlands, the back roads of Texas."

"Where else, Mr. President, where else?"

■ ■ ■

HE WOULDN'T BOTHER WITH TIM Seligman. He went right into the lion's mouth, called Ramona Dazzle at Rifkin, Rifkin & White.

"Ramona dear, you'll have to airlift the yellow bus. I'm going on a pilgrimage. . . . Yes, darling. And I'll need Michael. We can't leave him alone. He'll cave at the Waldorf. I'd prefer him with me. We'll reach out, Ramona, shake hands with Texas pioneers. Reporters will have a field day. The elitist president-elect working in the fields of West Texas . . . I'll need Marianna, too. You'll airlift her and Michael with the bus. . . . No, Clarice stays where she is. And no arguments, Ramona, or I'll jump ship and you'll have Michael on your hands."

Isaac had to close his entire shop. He couldn't have easy targets lying around while he was on the road. Marilyn would have to join him and Joey in Texas. But he was worried about Margaret Tolstoy. David Pearl might wreak vengeance on Isaac's loved ones if he lost all his bets and couldn't convert his acreage in the Bronx into hard cash. But Isaac couldn't airlift Margaret from her sanitarium near the Cloisters. He got Bull Latham on the horn.

"Bull, we have to talk."

"What about right now?"

"We can't yatter on the horn, you dummy."

"Meet me downstairs. I'm at the Brazos Barn. It's an enchilada joint five minutes from the Warwick."

"You followed me to Houston?"

"Wouldn't be much of a Bureau, Mr. President, if we couldn't anticipate your moves."

Trevor Welles didn't want Isaac to leave the room. "I can't protect, sir, out there in Indian country."

"I won't fall on any buffalo bricks. I'm five minutes away."

And Isaac lit out of the Warwick, into a sea of hot wind that smelled like a late autumn sirocco.

17

THE BIG GUY SWELLED WITH anger. He was prodded and fucked at every side, as if he were some mechanical cow, or the toy of Bull Latham at the FBI. The Bull and his men must have been right behind Isaac at the airport, with schnozzolas of their own. But the Bull didn't have to wear a schnoz. He had his own fortress, a phalanx of men, with their blue field jackets and fiberglass vests. They were as hairy as his old football team and could overwhelm an airport, a rodeo, or half the towns in Texas.

Isaac wasn't worried. He sailed right into the sirocco and found the Brazos Barn. It served tacos and white wine and was twice as expensive as the Bull's own haunt at the Waldorf. It was Tex-Mex with a Houston twist, a converted barn with a zinc bar as long as a runway. The Bull seemed happy there. Nobody gave a damn that he ran the FBI. People recognized him from his days with the Cowboys. And they also recognized the Big Guy. But they left him and the Bull alone. Isaac didn't see one of Bull Latham's lads in their fucking field jackets and whiter than white shirts that could burn a hole in your head.

The Bull was smiling like a little boy. "Thanks, Mr. President . . . for picking me as your running mate."

Isaac was appalled. "You bugged General MacArthur's rooms, listened to my talk with the DNC? I could have you thrown in jail."

The Bull was still smiling. "Isaac, we listen to everybody and everything."

"But it was just a ploy," Isaac said. "I wanted to hit Ramona Dazzle where it hurts."

"It's the sentiment that counts, Mr. President."

"Don't you bet against Michael. He'll be living at the White House, not me."

"It no longer matters. He's damaged beyond repair. The more you prop him up, the harder he'll fall. . . . What can I do for you, Mr. President?"

"I want Margaret Tolstoy to have protection around the clock."

"It's already been done. Nobody gets to see her, nobody. But I'd be careful, Mr. President. I wouldn't trust Trevor Welles. He switches friends faster than a Tijuana whore."

The Big Guy must have been going out of his mind. He could picture a Tijuana whore with Inez's helmet of silver hair. And he had to hide the erection in his pocket. And this was the lad who was going to swerve around a constitutional crisis—Isaac Sidel of Manhattan and the Bronx.

"But Joey swears by Trevor Welles. I have to trust my own son-in-law."

"Not if he was ever a Crusader. They're killers, Mr. President, killers sworn to themselves, with their own mad loyalty oaths. And I can't lay a finger on them. They're all tied to some government agency, with clearance all way up to God and the White House— what should I do about Clarice?"

"Nothing," Isaac said. "The country doesn't care about her. She can't compromise J. Michael, whatever she does. She wouldn't have much currency with a kidnapper."

"And what about your wife?"

"Ah," Isaac said, "the Countess Kathleen." She was an Irish beauty from Marble Hill. Isaac had married her when he was nineteen. She had smoothed his way with the Irish chieftains at the NYPD, or Isaac would never have risen so fast. He couldn't have maneuvered without Kathleen. But she abandoned him and Marilyn, moved to Florida and bought up real estate in Miami and Key West. He could still remember the taste of her wild red hair. When he first met Kathleen, it seemed as if her scalp was like a forest fire. He'd always been dazzled by those wondrous maidens of Marble Hill, redheads who could devour whole bushels of men, swallow them with their Guinness. He might have been faithful to Kathleen all his life, or was it another one of Isaac's big lies? She ran from him as he rose in the ranks, left him her bank account. Had she cuckolded Isaac, been in love with another man all the years they were together? But perhaps his own memory had gone south, and he'd humiliated Kathleen, shoved her away. No reporters could get to Kathleen. She wouldn't give any interviews about that bearish husband of hers. She'd withdrawn into her Miami mansion, a millionairess many times over. She hadn't even come to Marilyn's wedding at Gracie Mansion, hadn't seen her own daughter marry Vietnam Joe. But Marilyn had had nine or ten other husbands. The Big Guy could no longer keep count.

"Bull, I don't think you have to worry about Kathleen. There are enough retired cops in Miami to fight off whatever mavericks might want to hurt me."

"Isaac, I'll still be her guardian angel and she'll never know. But watch your back when you're in alligator country with Trevor Welles."

Isaac stared across the zinc bar. "Are there a whole lot of alligators between here and El Paso?"

"Miles and miles of them," said the Bull. "And some gator could come out of the bayou and bite your ass off."

"That would humble a man. I'd have to attend Michael's coronation in a wheelchair."

And he ran out of the Brazos Barn before the Bull could say
another word. He was always running now, but he couldn't recall his
destination from one moment to the next.

■ ■ ■

THE BULL JUST SAT THERE. Even if he had the manpower, he wouldn't
arrest half the planet to safeguard one reckless man. Sidel loved to tilt
against windmills as Manhattan's Don Quixote. And the Bull wasn't
going to play his Sancho Panza. He himself had to tilt between President Cottonwood and the Pentagon. He also had to stroke David
Pearl—the president was nothing more than David's little man. And the
president-elect was even more beholden to David. Cottonwood was a
devious cocksucker, but Michael was a crook. Michael had sold himself
to whatever whore was around. The Bull had a file on him that couldn't
even fit into a vault. Michael would never even get past his honeymoon
period. There would be no honeymoon for J. Michael Storm.

The phone rang at the Brazos Barn. It was the Bull's secure line.
He had ten or twenty lines like that around the country, lines that
couldn't be traced, since their signals were scrambled by his own
technicians at the Bureau.

He could hear the purring of David Pearl. But the old man
seemed agitated.

"Latham, I could have Cottonwood pull you right out of your seat."

The Bull smiled as he copied from Mr. Ansonia and purred into
the phone. "And why would you do that, David?"

"Because Sidel is out of control."

"But that's your fault. The minute he's about to land on his ass,
you prop him up."

"I can't help it," David rasped. "He's my protégé. But I'd rather he
never leaves Texas—alive or dead."

"Sir," the Bull said, "I pity the man who does Isaac in. You'll haunt him into the grave with your own wrath. I'm not prepared to pay that price."

"Go on. Be his altar boy. But don't you interfere with the plans I have for Isaac."

And the Bull's secure line went dead. He grabbed a few salted almonds from a bowl. He was in no hurry. Until Isaac climbed aboard his yellow wagon train, Bull had nowhere else to go.

18

I T WAS WELL PAST MIDNIGHT. Isaac was in the lobby of the Warwick, mooning over a glass of milk. He sat behind a potted plant,
where no one could intrude upon his privacy. And she wandered
into his field of vision wearing that same backless blue dress she'd
enticed him with at Cassandra's Wall. It was another bit of make-
believe. The woman he adored was all decoration. *I love you*, she'd
written. *Leave me alone.* And he did.

She sat with five men in the lobby, laughing and drinking.
How could he not listen to that luscious roar of hers, the growl of
her voice? It echoed under the Warwick's chandeliers. Of all the
hotels in Houston, she had to pick his. But he didn't need Sherlock
Holmes' guidebook to tell him that she'd come here on purpose, to
eat his heart out. Isaac couldn't even appraise the five men. Were
they generals, assassins, captains of industry, or actors playing
their own cruel parts?

She didn't trot off with any of them. She left these five clowns
and wandered across the Warwick's endless lobby. Isaac followed
her into that labyrinth. It was as complicated as the Houston Ship

Channel. He caught Inez as she was about to enter a tiny corridor. She wasn't even startled to see the Big Guy. He should have kissed her and shut up, but he was too delirious.

"Did David send you here?"

"Yes and no," she said. "I'm his eyes and ears."

"Just like Eleanor Roosevelt. She went into coal mines for FDR, and you've come to the Warwick."

"Isaac," she said, "run home before Texas becomes your tombstone."

"I can't. But I could steal you from the old man and take you into the bayous. We'll ride on an alligator's back."

She laughed, but that deep growl had gone out of her voice.

"Darling, it's too late for alligators."

He wanted to hit her, but he would have broken himself, not Inez. He appealed to her like a rat-poor minstrel.

"Stay with me tonight, and I won't bother you again."

She fondled his ears. "Isaac, we already had our honeymoon . . . at the Ansonia. And I can't afford a second one."

She shoved right past Sidel. He didn't have the heart to stop her. If he had to have a tombstone, he wanted to share it with Inez. Texas couldn't have been as deep a heart of darkness as the Bronx. He wouldn't rush home. The Big Guy would have to be more vigilant than he'd ever been.

■ ■ ■

IT PAINED HER TO SEE his shoulders slump. She was no longer certain whether the mask she wore belonged to Trudy or Inez. Perhaps she was the monster who had been bitten by her many names. She watched the big bear shuffle across the carpets. There wasn't much sense in loving him. She loved him anyway. What would happen to Daniel and Darl if she moved close to Isaac and his crazy fire?

Ah, she was Inez tonight, Inez in a blue dress, and she didn't have to think of how her identities spiraled back and forth. She returned to the lobby. The barman had come to her with a telephone. But she sent him back to the bar. All she had to do was wait.

He arrived around three in the morning with that linebacker's grace of his. Bull Latham had always been light on his feet. He had half a dozen of his acolytes—men and women with bland faces and brutal eyes. They could have cracked her spine before she ever blinked.

The Bull sat down next to her. He had a bottle of Jameson in his coat pocket. Would he drink them both into oblivion or douse Inez in whiskey and set her on fire inside the Warwick?

"Inez, you've been a naughty girl. You had no license to come here."

"But I had the names of some generals in my head. They were happy to meet with David's social secretary. I had a delightful chat with them. They're going to stuff the Bronx inside their shoes and shuttle between Houston and Claremont Park."

The Bull took out his Jameson and drank right from the bottle. "That doesn't concern you," he said.

"It might not if Isaac Sidel didn't have to be sacrificed."

The Bull looked into her brown eyes. He wasn't half as cruel as his own acolytes. "Sidel is a luxury you can't afford. I could put you on a cargo plane and ship you back to the Ansonia in a dog kennel. David says he can't sleep unless you're on the thirteenth floor."

"Tough," she said.

But he knew how to menace her without his bottle of whiskey. "Did I tell you how I visited Darl's school?"

"Shut up," she said.

"David has appointed me her godfather. It ain't every little gal who can share a milkshake with the director of the FBI. You're a delinquent mother who cohabited with criminals in New Orleans. I can send Daniel and Darl into the courts, and they'll be lost in the maze. You'll never see your kids again."

Inez reached out to scratch his face, but he laughed and clutched both her hands inside his paw.

"Don't you ever go near my Darl again," she spat at him.

"Why, she's just about the prettiest gal in creation. She's a pure delight. . . . And you listen to me. Stop meddling in Sidel's business. You signed on with David, and I'm here to see that you stay signed."

She didn't even resist. She had no more feeling in her fingers. The Bull released them from his paw. She'd been on a fool's journey. She flirted with the generals, tried to wean them away from the Bronx, but she did Isaac more harm than good. The generals had called David, who sent a distress signal to Bull Latham. Bull was both the puppet and the puppeteer. He did David's bidding, but he had to be cautious around Sidel. Who knows? A miracle could happen, and Isaac might survive his Texas tombstone. So she winked at Bull's acolytes and walked out of the Warwick with the FBI.

19

H E'D BECOME A KIND OF prince regent in the wake of a falter-
ing king. No one listened to Michael, or bothered to inter-
rogate him, but he was the president-elect, not Sidel. The
yellow bus arrived on a cargo plane the very next afternoon. But
Isaac had to wait for Marilyn, Marianna, and Michael. It was near
the holiday season, and Marianna would only miss nine or ten days
of school. But the Big Guy was adamant; he found her a Texas tutor
and charged the tutor's bill to the DNC. He didn't know how Marilyn and Marianna would get along, but they were already like sisters
conspiring against Isaac Sidel.

It was hard for Michael. His own advisers deferred to the Big
Guy. But it was even harder for Martin Boyle, who'd arrived on the
same plane with Michael. Boyle had fallen out of favor. He could
barely get an interview with the Big Guy, who didn't even have to
depend on Trevor Welles and his Crusaders. He had his own "secret
service," detectives from Barbarossa's old squad, burly men who
guarded the mayor when he was on the road.

And while Martin Boyle brooded, Isaac went up to him and

kissed his forehead, like some kind of pontiff. "How much did David Pearl pay you, huh?'"

"Not a dime. I serve my country. I can't be bought."

"Shut your fucking mouth, Boyle, or I'll flay you alive—no, I'll have my son-in-law do it. That's what he did to the Vietcong."

The Secret Service man swayed on his feet, like some crooner, but he had little to croon about. "Calder promised you wouldn't get hurt."

"You were sworn to protect me, Boyle, not to become a rat in my own camp."

"Then why haven't you kicked me off the detail?"

"Because you're part of my family now, and I can't discard my own bad sons. But if you betray me again, Boyle, I'll have you pensioned off without a pension. You'll have to beg like a blind man . . . get the fuck out of my sight."

The yellow bus took to the back roads. They went through a town of shanties that wasn't even on the map; it was a colored ghetto on a forgotten hump of prairie grass between Houston and Corpus Christi. The children never even bothered about Isaac. They were in awe of the Little First Lady. Marianna went into a shack and baked butternut cookies for the entire town. There wasn't a school or a library that Isaac could see.

"We have to fix this place," Isaac said to one of the town fathers. "Mayor to mayor."

"We don't need fixin', Mr. Isaac," said the mayor of this very visible invisible town. And he pointed to the television cameras and the reporters who had wandered into his dusty landscape with Isaac's yellow bus. "And we sure as hell don't need the damn publicity of politicians who have nothin' better to do than ramble in the dust. We're in love with the Little First Lady, but we'd rather love her from afar. Do you get my drift?"

"But we've come to help," Isaac said like a supplicant.

"Sir, it's better for us that white folks aren't so aware that we exist—no neighbors are the best neighbors, that's my opinion. We were near decimated a while back by our white neighbors. We pay taxes, even vote at the votin' booth in Goliad. But that's as much traffic as we can bear. . . . Be gone, Mr. Isaac."

And the Big Guy had to drag his tail out of there. He wondered what other town he might ruin with his entourage. He passed through the craziest place he had ever seen, a ghost town filled with books rather than people. It was run by some lunatic bibliophile, who lived and bathed among his mountains of books. He welcomed the Pilgrimage of '88, as this Democratic whirlwind was now called by the press. His name was Carter Greenhut. He'd made a fortune manipulating stocks and bonds and now withdrew into a wonderland of books. He had neither wife nor child, not even a pet alligator on a leash. He survived with just a servant-cook, who repaired broken pipes, fixed Carter's meals, and had to drive fifty miles to the nearest 7-Eleven.

"Armageddon is a-coming," said the bibliophile. "And I have to prepare for the prince of darkness."

"With a battlefield of books?" Isaac asked.

"Satan is frightened of the Word. . . . The printed page can blind him."

And Isaac wondered if Carter Greenhut had come out of the same mental ward as that shooter Billy Bob. He drank a cup of tea with Carter that had all the delight of tepid alligator piss and had to fly from the town of books before he himself went mad. Perhaps the Big Guy could outrun his own Armageddon. He wasn't so sure. The people who lined the back roads waiting for the Democratic ticket had the look of the damned; they had reddish, raw eyes and mumbled to themselves. Isaac had to feed them whatever food he had.

He couldn't really sniff the lay of the land. Something was wrong. It was too fucking allegorical, this descent into darkness. A little hamlet of poor blacks that seemed outside the usual rub of time, and another hamlet, bereft of people, where the only real citizens were books. Isaac might have been less suspicious if he'd seen one live alligator. But it was as if their little caravan of Democrats was trapped inside the brainstorm of a wizard in a limestone castle. . . .

They slept in motels among the bayous or in some dead orchard, where they could park the yellow bus. Isaac had his own bungalow. But it couldn't protect him from having the same bad dream. A boy again, in short pants, he was bumping along when he discovered a cafeteria right on Broadway, with electric signboards above his head. The women painted on them were twenty feet tall. They looked ready to leap out of the signboards and crush a boy in short pants.

He ran into the cafeteria, but he had to pay a premium of fifty cents if he wanted to sit at one of the tables. These tables were much too tall, and the chairs were treacherous. It took him the better part of an hour to find his way onto a bruised leather seat. And he couldn't command any of the waiters no matter how hard he signaled. He didn't have an ounce of pedigree inside this cafeteria. No one would listen. He began to sob.

And then he saw her. She sat next to Isaac in a tall chair. But she wasn't harsh and overweening, like the women in the signboards. She had a silver hat clapped to her head. He wished it were Trudy Winckleman, come to haunt his nights in a humdrum motel. But this cafeteria lady had very long legs. And then he recognized her. He was looking at the original Inez, Rothstein's blond beauty, but what was Inez doing in a strange cafeteria, with a silver hat that some conquistador might have worn? This wasn't Lindy's, where Legs Diamond walked from front to rear, as a warning to anyone who welshed on a bet with the Brain or forgot the interest on a loan. Isaac couldn't even sample some sauerkraut.

Inez heard his stomach growl. She bent over him like one of those colossal ladies in the signboards and patted his eyes with a napkin. He was certain that Inez would sit him on her lap and feed him something from the counter, which was very far away, or at least whistle at a waiter. But the dream always ended with Inez stuffing the napkin—a rag, really—into his mouth until Isaac could no longer breathe.

And he'd wake out of this nightmare in some no-man's-land between Texas and the Ansonia, wishing he'd never, never agreed to become the nation's VP.

■ ■ ■

IT WASN'T THAT MUCH BETTER during the day. He was tied to a yellow bus on a pilgrimage he didn't believe in. He had to protect his loved ones, who traveled with him on a sinister route.

The villages and hamlets they visited along the Gulf had been half-destroyed by some hurricane; the restaurants were shuttered; the gas stations had no gas. Children stared at them from cardboard windows. They could have been born in the Bronx. "Jesus," Isaac said to Michael. "Will you take some notes? We'll have to come back here after the inauguration and help these forgotten people."

"There won't be an inauguration," Michael moaned. He had fallen into a drunken stupor since their first day on the road. Isaac cursed himself. He had to swallow dust and drink alligator piss just because the Constitution had neglected to deal with a president-elect who ran from his own election before Congress and the Electoral College could ratify him. But the College did convene in all fifty states while the yellow bus approached the wetlands of some lost lagoon. And the votes cast by the College with its own strange mystique would be sent on to the Capitol in DC and remain unanswered and unopened until Congress itself convened in January to count the electoral votes and declare who had really won the election. Until then, the Big Guy and Michael would have to diddle around in the wetlands and backwoods.

But suddenly, their yellow bus had become the Little White House. Senators and congressmen arrived in that lost lagoon, Democrats and Republicans alike, to pay homage to the new powerhouse, Isaac Sidel. Michael wasn't even mentioned. A clique of senators wanted Isaac's opinion on a particular appropriations bill. Others asked him whether he might consider having a woman as secretary of state. Isaac was saddled with a transition team, in spite of himself. He tried to defer all questions to the president-elect, but no one wanted Michael.

Isaac had to pose with his own first family. None of the reporters had ever seen Marilyn before. She wasn't shy in front of the cameras. She said that her father was a little too free with his Glock. And Isaac sulked over his son-in-law. All of Joey's dealing in Saigon would soon come out. But the Big Guy posed with Marilyn, Joe, and the Little First Lady, while Michael sat like some deranged Ajax in his "tent," which was the very last seat of the bus.

Isaac always mentioned Michael first, kept insisting on "Storm-Sidel," but the reporters only heard *his* name. He had already been crowned by them, right in the middle of the bayous. And then Mr. Death, Trevor Welles, drifted through all of Isaac's bodyguards and brought the secretary of defense onto the bus, Mr. Sumner Mars of Idaho. He was one of the richest men in America and had his own ranch near Bald Mountain. He wore a western string tie and a rancher's boots. Mars was forty-five years old, with the rugged looks of a mountaineer. He nearly crushed one of Isaac's knuckles with his iron grip. The Big Guy had to struggle to get his hand back.

"Mr. President, there's been a terrible blunder. I blame myself. Some ambitious officers in San Antone and elsewhere have been trawling around for the Pentagon, looking for new reservoirs of land. But they trawled behind my back. We have no business in the Bronx. We wouldn't build one of our bases in your backyard."

Now Isaac was deeply suspicious. Secretary Mars didn't have to make his own pilgrimage to the Democrats' Little White House in the middle of nowhere. He'd be returning to his ranch in a couple of weeks. What had possessed him to board the yellow bus? He'd never really been attached to the Republican Party or Texas financiers.

"Then I have your word?" Isaac said, offering Mars his last cold

Dr Pepper. "Because if there is a sudden land grab, Mr. Secretary, I'll ruffle every fucking feather you have."

Mars never blinked. "I'll ruin the man who dispossesses one Latino family in the Bronx."

The Big Guy was troubled more than ever. His left arm began to twitch. He let Mars pump his hand again, said good-bye, and sought out his son-in-law. "Joey, something stinks. If the cap pistols start going off, grab Marilyn and Marianna and run for the hills."

"Dad, there aren't any hills."

"I have this funny feeling. I think we're all sitting ducks."

"So do I."

"Are the Crusaders dealing against us?"

"If they are, Dad, then it's my fault. But Colonel Welles didn't ever let me down, not even once."

"He's still Mr. Death."

Meanwhile, Isaac's wagon train grew smaller and smaller. TV stations recalled their crews. Reporters disappeared one by one, having been pulled onto meatier assignments. Not even Isaac and Marianna could entertain America after their first week on the road. And ten minutes after he told Trevor Welles to break up this entourage and abandon the tour of Texas, the bus had two flat tires. They were stranded in Zapata County, ten miles from the Mexican border, in some strange foothill that overlooked a field of mesquite. Was this a momentary reprieve? Would they drag him to El Paso and snuff him out in one of the back alleys, where gangs from Tijuana with Glocks of their own were waiting for him? Would it be like having a taste of Saigon?

He could hear the blades of a whirlybird. He thought the Prez had come to visit him on *Marine One*. But it wasn't Calder Cottonwood. This bird didn't have the seal of the United States. It was a Chinook that had no markings and had been painted black. A dozen men scrambled out of the bird before it hit the ground. They wore combat boots and night-fighter paint, were dressed in black and carried machine pistols or deer slayers—Mossberg Mountaineers. Isaac groaned to himself as he recognized Billy Bob Archer under that paint.

"Run," he whispered to Joey. "With the two girls."

"Dad, it's too late."

The Big Guy's bodyguards had drawn their Glocks.

"Children," he said, "put your toys away. They'll tear us to pieces."

But Martin Boyle stood in front of Isaac and Marianna, and aimed his .22 Magnum at Trevor Welles.

"Boyle," Isaac said, "will you put it down, for fuck's sake? You're trying to get the drop on Mr. Death."

"I don't care," Boyle said. But he never had the chance to say another word. Billy Bob shot him between the eyes with his deer slayer. Marianna stifled a scream. But she couldn't take her eyes off Martin Boyle, who died without twitching once.

"That's enough," Isaac said while Joe Barbarossa whispered in his ear.

"Dad, let me negotiate with these mothers."

Isaac started to blubber. "You can't negotiate with Mr. Death. They'll do the same to you."

But Vietnam Joe pinched his father-in-law and glanced at Mr. Death.

"You shouldn't have lied to me, Colonel Trevor."

"Joey, did I have a choice? You would have skinned us alive if we didn't get you out into the open with the Big Guy. We'd never have gotten past your white glove."

"What do you want?"

"That depends. You wore the Crusaders' badge. You were one of us. It would grieve me to pop out your lights. You can walk away with the Big Guy's daughter, but you have to promise not to tattle on us."

"Stop it," Joey said. "We wouldn't get very far, not while your freelancers are carrying half a dozen deer slayers.

"Freelancers?" said Trevor Welles. "That wounds me to the

quick. We're patriots. We protect the president of the United States and all his interests."

"There is no fucking United States while you and your lunatics roam around in your Chinook," Isaac said. "Why don't you protect Michael? Isn't he the president-elect?"

"We are protecting him. Aren't we, Mikey?"

The wounded warrior stepped out of the yellow bus. This is the Michael that Isaac should have remembered, the double-dealer of double-dealers. There was no pain in his eyes, no remorse.

"Michael," Isaac said. "Forget about me. They'll kill your own daughter."

"No, they won't. We'll keep her in storage, hide her in some ranch."

"Yeah," Isaac said, "some ranch in Idaho, right under Bald Mountain. . . . It's all about Sidereal, isn't it? You were always Pearl's partner. And you brought in the Prez. He's as moral as a cockroach—a Texas cockroach. You and your Texas partners will make a killing."

"Without me," said the Little First Lady, who leapt on Michael and bit his arm. He howled, but Marianna clung to him until Trevor Welles tossed her into the mesquite. Isaac picked her out of the gnarled branches, rocked her in his arms, and scowled at Michael.

"Jesus, you're the one who's the real Mr. Death. The others are just paid clerks."

"Are you calling me a clerk, Mr. Fancy Pants?" asked Billy Bob, who licked the barrel of his Mossberg Mountaineer, like some madcap Davy Crockett.

"No, Billy Bob. But I doubt that you're God's eye. You don't even have the dignity of a little devil."

"Colonel Trevor," Billy Bob said, "are you gonna let Mr. Fancy Pants insult me? Then I'll do his daughter first."

"Shut up, Billy Bob."

"Then let me do Vietnam Joe. . . . I'm hungry to do it."

"Come on," Joe said, edging toward Michael. "I'll rip this Judas off at the neck before you get near me."

But Billy Bob hit him with the butt of his deer slayer before he could lunge at Michael. Joey spun around once and fell into Isaac's arms. "Dad," he said, "I'm sorry," and drifted into his own dark dream. Isaac sang the mourner's song deep inside his head. He didn't mind taking a bullet. But he didn't want Marilyn and Joey to die. And he refused to imagine a world where Marianna couldn't grow up. They'd give her a horse to ride on at Sumner Mars' ranch. And then they'd realize she was too dangerous to have around. First they'd put her in some cage in the ground, and they'd strangle her soon enough.

But his mind began to explode. He had an erection while the slaughter was about to begin. He couldn't stop thinking of Inez's silver crown. He was getting delirious with the aroma of her armpits. She'd tried to warn him in Houston after David had planned his caper with Mr. Death. The Big Guy hadn't listened, hadn't even caressed her silver hair. Would they hurl the yellow bus down a ravine and swear it was an unholy accident? And Michael would mourn the death of his running mate.

Ah, but at least Marilyn had settled in with a man. That was one consolation. She'd been in love with Isaac's adjutant, Manfred Coen, and he'd driven Manfred toward his own slaughter. Marilyn's many marriages had been her own revenge against her dad. But she loved Joey, perhaps because he reminded her of Coen. They both had the shyness of born killers, even if Manfred had never killed anyone.

He wouldn't shut his eyes. He wanted to drift through hell with his eyes open.

But he was startled when Billy Bob's head split like a pumpkin and his brains splattered all over Isaac. He didn't even hear the noise of a gun. The Crusaders never had a chance to hide behind the bus. Trevor Welles was the last to fall. He lay with all his freelancers dressed in black. Aside from the bits of brain all over him, Isaac didn't see much blood. But he could have been misled. All that sudden commotion had created a dust storm in a matter of minutes.

Then the dust cleared, and Bull Latham came down off the foothills, with a scatter of agents in field jackets right behind him. He wasn't even carrying a firearm.

"Sharpshooters, huh? Isaac, those guys weren't shit."

"You bugged the bus, didn't you, Bull?"

"Mr. President, how could I leave a baby like you all alone in the desert? Should I cuff that son of a bitch, J. Michael Storm? He's the Bureau's biggest catch."

"No," Isaac said. "Michael is mine."

He hugged Marilyn and Marianna and started to cry. "Will you cover up Martin Boyle, huh, Bull? I don't want him to rot like that. And call an ambulance for my son-in-law. He's hurt. Jesus, does a guy have to do everything for himself?"

PART FIVE

20

H E HADN'T RETURNED WHOLE FROM the hinterland. Texas had scratched him in some fundamental way. His brow was pierced with dark lines. He could have been Manhattan's own Mr. Hyde. All he wanted to do was hit and hit and hit. But Isaac couldn't create another constitutional crisis. Those who had survived the shootout near Zapata, Texas, had been sworn to secrecy. He wanted to knock on Inez's door, howl until she heard him. He almost did. But Isaac seemed to harm whoever was near. He had to maneuver beneath his fierce brow.

He left Secretary Mars in place. But he still chopped at the Pentagon. Bull Latham said that a maverick society of elite troops, under the cover of the medical center at Fort Sam Houston, had plotted to murder the president-elect and his running mate. The plotters had worked alone. Several of them were patients or former patients at Fort Sam's psychiatric wing.

Reporters pounced on the story and wouldn't let it lie dead. They kept looking for possible coconspirators, but they couldn't even get near the president-elect. He was locked inside his suite at the Waldorf and never even left the hotel. The Big Guy would have him in handcuffs if he ever walked out onto the street. President Cottonwood had a memorial service for Martin Boyle in the Rose Garden, with a marine honor guard and a coffin draped in an American flag. "That's the least I can do for one of my own boys who fell in the line of duty."

But Isaac wouldn't attend the memorial for his own Secret Service man. He boycotted the Rose Garden and President Cottonwood. Reporters could smell a feud between the United States and New York. Isaac held his own memorial outside Gracie Mansion, with an honor guard from the NYPD. The president's chopper interrupted the service. *Marine One* landed on the winter grass, and Cottonwood climbed out. The Big Guy wouldn't shake his hand. Reporters realized that Cottonwood meant very little in the fiefdom of Manhattan. He was one more superfluous man.

Isaac wept during the service. Martin Boyle hadn't been a bad man. He was caught up in the president's own intrigue and died because of it, in some crazy battle for broken land in the Bronx. After the service, the Prez followed Isaac like a puppy onto the back porch of the mansion.

The Big Guy wouldn't even offer him a cupcake or a butternut cookie—Marianna had again become the mistress of Gracie Mansion. No one talked about *Lolita*. It was better that the Big Guy wasn't alone. And Marianna did have a chaperone, Amanda Wilde, even though Isaac knew she wasn't worth shit.

"Son," Cottonwood said, "what can I do to make amends?"

"As a starter, you can stay out of Manhattan and the Bronx. And if you meddle one more time, I'll collar you myself the moment you vacate the White House."

"Understood," said the Prez, still the same puppy dog.

"There's no more Sidereal, no more dream of a gigantic circus tent in the Bronx. You'll give up whatever holdings you have.

You'll pluck all the generals out of the air force base in San Antone and have them retire before you leave office. And you'll bring in an entirely new team at the Fort Sam medical center. If there's one more deal under the table, I'll march right into the Oval Office and rip your heart out."

"Understood."

"Now get your ass back onto your whirlybird, and keep the fuck away from me."

Reporters watched Calder lean into the wind of *Marine One* and vanish into the sky. They realized that there was a new leader of the Western World, and he had no rivals. The president of France wanted to meet with Sidel. "I'm flattered," Isaac told the reporters stationed in Room Nine at City Hall. "But I'm only Michael Storm's running mate. I have a city to run, and I shouldn't be climbing onto a bigger stage."

But his denials made little difference. Journalists from all over the planet crowded into Room Nine. The Little First Lady was on the cover of *Paris Match*. And there was a very long article in *Die Zeit* about the sudden sea change in American politics. "There has never been a mayor before like Isaac Sidel. He rules Manhattan with a Glock in his pants, like some desperado who has become America's new marshal. The rivalry between Houston and Manhattan runs very deep. Houston itself was founded by a pair of New Yorkers, the Allen brothers, land speculators who bought up Buffalo Bayou and named their new town after General Sam Houston, commander in chief of the Republic of Texas. And now the Sun Belt may have a Manhattan general as the nation's new commander in chief."

The Big Guy gave no interviews. He rode into the Bronx with a caravan of bodyguards from the NYPD. The Secret Service sat at the rear of this caravan. Isaac stood in all the debris, like some King Kong on a mountain of rubble, while all the cameras clicked. There wasn't much ambiguity. When it came to the Bronx, Isaac was king of the hill.

Then he rode downtown to NYU Medical Center, where Joe Bar-barossa lay in a private room, having been flown in from a hospital in Laredo. His son-in-law had a fractured skull.

"Dad," Joey said, "I'm sorry I let you down."

"Come on," Isaac said, "you rescued us. You stalled the Crusad-ers, let Bull Latham have a couple of extra minutes, so he could shoot the shit out of Trevor Welles."

"But I should have been more alert to Trevor's tricks."

"Ah, it was Saigon all over again, a land of double-dealers."

He discovered Marilyn in the waiting room. His only daughter had lost that wild, rebellious looks of hers. She was very pale. And the Big Guy couldn't help himself. He was riven with a terrifying guilt. He'd been that way ever since Manfred Coen had died in a Ping-Pong parlor while Isaac was a lowly inspector who battled a family of pimps in the Bronx. Isaac had tossed Coen into the battle and got him killed. Manfred's blue eyes still haunted him.

"I'm sorry," he said. "I should have let you live with Blue Eyes. . . . "

"Papa," she said, "if you want absolution, you won't get it from me."

He almost grinned behind his tears. Marilyn's wildness had come back. He didn't want her to forgive him. The Big Guy preferred to suffer.

"Just take care of Joe," she said. "And keep him away from your shenanigans."

He pecked her on the cheek. That was the only kind of kiss she would accept from her embattled father. But something rubbed at him, remained raw. Joey had a broken head, and Martin Boyle was a ghost, because of some fucking land grab that involved Cottonwood, Michael, Sumner Mars, a fistful of generals and Texas tycoons, and David Pearl, with his gangsters and soldiers of fortune, like the Cru-saders. But why hadn't Bull Latham whacked the Crusaders before Martin Boyle was killed? Why didn't he stop that yellow bus while it was stranded in some lost Texas town of black citizens? And couldn't he have captured a couple of Crusaders without killing them all?

Bull Latham wasn't at the Waldorf. Isaac had him get on an afternoon shuttle out of DC. They met at the Bull & Bear, sat at its magnificent eight-cornered mahogany bar, where businessmen could suck on their whiskey-and-water and watch the tiny ribbon of rising and falling stocks on the restaurant wall. Isaac had nothing to invest in the market.

Even as mayor, he paid no attention to its rise and fall. The city's money managers had to deal behind his back.

Isaac sipped a glass of milk while Bull had his own bottle of Jameson whiskey. Isaac adored that green bottle with its tiny indented bell at the bottom.

He smiled his friendliest smile, clinked glasses, and said, "Bull, your whole fucking career depends on this discussion. Lie to me now, and you'll walk into an endless shitstorm."

The Bull humped his linebacker's shoulders. "Mr. Mayor, are you threatening me?"

"Yes."

And the Bull started to laugh. "Then I'd better not tape our little tête-à-tête."

"How much did Pearl pay you to whack Trevor Welles and all his men?"

The Bull munched on some peanuts from a bowl. "Isaac, recall. I saved your ass."

"But you could have prevented me from going on that trip."

"I'm no Cassandra," he said. "I can't predict. I went with the flow."

"You must have sensed how Trevor was choreographing things. Dragging us through one little nightmare of a town after the other, until the journalists and their camera crews dropped away. He had to prepare for our little accident. David Pearl wanted me dead."

"Yeah, but I couldn't pounce until Trevor made his move."

"And you decided to do a little business," Isaac said.

"But it didn't change the complexion of things. The Crusaders had to go. I got the old man on the horn and asked him for a bonus."

"A bonus? For whacking the vice president–elect?"

"Yeah, he would have liked that. But he couldn't persuade me. Besides, there was a little hesitation in his voice—he's fond of you, calls you his protégé. But if I was going to silence the Crusaders, he wanted it clean as a whistle. I probably would have done it anyway. I had to finish off Trevor and his little band. No one could have taken them alive. And they might have hurt Marilyn."

"Stuff it, Bull. You got your bonus, and I won't even ask how much it is. But don't start acting like some morality king. You're a bigger son of a bitch than I'll ever be."

The Bull poured from his green bottle. "I'll take that as a compliment."

"But if you ever side with that old man again, if you so much as wink at him, I'll whisper in Cottonwood's ear. And he'll collapse your whole tent. I have him by the balls. And all your bugs and million-dollar mikes aren't going to save Pearl. It's total war, Bull. Keep out of my way."

Isaac left him there with his green bottle and marched right out of the Waldorf.

■ ■ ■

HE WAS HAUNTED IN HIS very own house. His only solace at Gracie Mansion was Marianna Storm. And yet the mansion was full of spies—it was crawling with Secret Service men, and there was also that star clerk, Amanda Wilde. So he kidnapped Marianna out of the kitchen and went up with her to his own heart of darkness, that wasteland of the Bronx. The Big Guy drove her in his sedan. Why should he be so fond of a twelve-year-old girl? Marianna was like a fellow conspirator. She would have been a fabulous secretary of state. And both of them had that sad demean of orphans. It almost seemed worse for Marianna that her parents were still alive. They were ruthless beyond repair. Isaac and Marianna would both suffer with Michael and Clarice in the White House.

Marianna was in love with her delinquent from the Bronx, Angel Carpenteros, who was much too controversial for the Democrats. He'd disappeared from her life, and now Marianna blamed the Big Guy.

"Uncle Isaac, will I ever see Angel again?"

"Not until your father's in the White House, or the DNC will have our heads."

"Papa doesn't belong there," she muttered. "And why should Angel have to suffer because of lunatics like him and Clarice?"

Ah, it's politics, Isaac wanted to say. But he had no answer, and he wouldn't lie to Marianna Storm. They stopped at Claremont Village, a monolithic world of housing projects that was one more moonscape in the Bronx. And yet Isaac felt comfortable in this outland. He was frightened that it wouldn't survive. The Pentagon wanted to build its own moonscape, an Indian reservation without Indians and without a heart.

They got out of the car. A local gang surrounded them. Its members had little interest in Isaac or his Glock, since they had Glocks of their own. They were intrigued by Marianna.

"Little Mama, ain't we seen you before? You're Angel Carpenteros' old lady."

"I only wish," Marianna said, glaring at Isaac. She had to sign her name on their silk blouses. And then they scattered. Isaac was guilty as hell. But he couldn't free up Angel Carpenteros.

Another car appeared in these endless dunes. He recognized David's gunsels. But they couldn't whack him and Marianna right in front of Claremont Village's own little gangland. They wouldn't have left the Bronx alive. But Isaac looked closer into the car. It was carrying a passenger—Inez.

She stepped out of the car. The boldness of her beauty shivered Isaac's spine. Marianna couldn't take her eyes off Inez, who could have been the queen of chaos in her silver helmet. Marianna had never been so intimidated by another woman.

"Uncle Isaac," she growled, "aren't you going to introduce me to your lady, or will you leave me stranded?"

Inez smiled with that sensuous mouth of hers. "I'm only half his lady," she said.

"But that half is more than he's ever had."

And both of them laughed while Isaac tottered in the wind. They whispered to one another, and then Inez took Isaac's arm and led him deeper into that moonscape, far from David's gunsels.

"Darling," she said, "I had a hard time tracking you."

Isaac started to groan. He wished Inez would track him for the rest of his life. He'd wait another hundred years for it to happen.

"You ordered me to leave you alone," he blabbered like some Bronx attorney.

She continued to smile at him. "Darling, you know me. I'm a fickle girl."

Sidel couldn't help himself. He started to bawl under the watchful eyes of Marianna and the gunsels. He held Inez in his arms, could feel the thunder of his own heart. He danced with her in the dunes, floated like Fred Astaire. But he couldn't shut up.

"Inez, you talked about your children, said they were in danger."

Her heart beat within the Big Guy's embrace.

"They still are. But I missed your bald spot and your big ears."

His bitterness crept back. "Missed me so much that you brought your own death squad."

She was silent for a moment, but that vagabond of vagabonds could no longer read her smile. She slipped out of his embrace.

"Silly boy, the best way of fooling David is to perform right in front of his spies."

"But you could be his biggest spy," Isaac had to protest. He was confused, in love with a witch who was wound up in the ancient material of a museum. But she wasn't a witch. She was another one of David Pearl's casualties.

"Come back with me," Isaac said. "I don't care what pact you have with David. I'll keep you at Gracie Mansion."

"As your little love doll?"

"No," he said. "I won't even kiss you. Just stay with me—and Marianna."

"And David will hold my two babies as his hostages. It's not a deal I can live with."

"Then why did you come here?"

"I had to see you one last time. I've never been in love with such a crazy man. David will let you live—he promised—if you award the Bronx to him. He'll get you the White House. Just give him the Bronx."

Isaac's face darkened in the brutal sunlight. He wanted to run howling into that endless plain of projects.

"Then you are his agent. You're reading me his terms."

"He has no terms," she said. "I'm just trying to protect your sweet face."

And she brushed her hand against his cheek. The Big Guy trembled. His knees nearly collapsed out from under him. He started to sway like some kind of magic rabbi—the source of his magic was Inez.

"I'll break him," Isaac mumbled.

"And if you do, darling, you'll also break me. I'm wired up to that old man. . . . Couldn't you forget about the Bronx?"

"And have the generals force every living soul out from under their giant teepee? I'm the mayor. They can't rob my grocery store."

She was sobbing now. It wounded Isaac. He'd never seen tears in her eyes.

"Then I'll just have to mourn you while you're still alive."

She wandered toward the gunsels' car.

"Wait," he said. But she was gone. She drove away with that little, murderous band. Isaac drifted back to his own car like a dead man.

Marianna was bewildered. "Uncle, what did the beautiful lady want?"

"The Bronx."

"Then why didn't you give it to her?"

Isaac couldn't even explain. David had thrown Inez at him, or perhaps she'd thrown herself. She couldn't understand what these badlands meant. He'd watched the borough die and die. He'd rather see the worst housing project in creation, with all the mayhem and the drug wars, then that dead village the Pentagon imagined. And David must have realized how bitter it would be for Isaac. That's why he brought Inez into the equation. He wanted Inez to suck Isaac into some black hole. Perhaps she did love Isaac. He'd have leapt into a black hole with her, have abandoned politics, and whatever little pomp he had, including his own baseball team of stragglers and orphans. But he couldn't abandon the Bronx. He'd have to find a way to fight for Inez.

21

HE WOULDN'T INVADE THE ANSONIA with his bodyguards. It was a landmark, and half of Isaac's history was tied to that limestone castle. AR and the first Inez haunted his life. The second Inez haunted him much, much more. He went upstairs to that little museum. Isaac knocked and knocked. He searched for his little bundle of picks. The picks had never failed him, but he tried the Ansonia's brass knob. The door wasn't even locked. The Big Guy stole inside and began to whimper. The whole apartment had been picked. There was nothing but barren walls. Even the lampshades and lightbulbs were gone. The Big Guy felt he had been violated. He could almost hear the murmur of his heart.

He strode up to the seventeenth floor. But he couldn't even get beyond the stairwell. It was thick with David's own thugs. They couldn't have been lads from DC. They didn't have that usual government patina. Yet Isaac recalled none of them. They weren't part of Manhattan's modern Maf. They must have come from an old school Isaac couldn't remember.

"Hey, Big Guy, what do ya want?"

"I'm here to see Mr. Pearl," Isaac said.

"But Davey don't wanna see ya."

"Ask him again," Isaac said. "As a personal favor."

The thugs withdrew and came back to the stairwell. They didn't even pat Isaac down. They let him keep his Glock. That's how little they feared Isaac Sidel. They followed him into David's apartment, ducking their heads under the low ceiling, as Isaac did. David was there in his slippers and mangled sweater, but he wore an orange scarf, like one of the Tammany Hall tigers.

"David, why did you get rid of your museum?"

"To eat your heart out. . . . No, I put it all in a warehouse in the Bronx, right next to Robert Moses' highway. I have to lock horns with a crazy man like you, and you might have stolen all my treasures, out of spite."

"Stop it," Isaac said. "I never harmed you."

David began to cackle. He was performing for his thugs, who could have been phantoms out of AR's own era.

"Harmed me? You took my livelihood away. The Bronx was my centerpiece. That's why I bought and bought . . . "

"Where's Inez?"

"In the grave, where you can't find her."

The old man watched the Big Guy blanch. "Not her, stupid. *My* Inez. I had to get rid of the museum. That bitch with the silver hair was in love with you. I couldn't trust her."

"Where is she, David?"

"Trudy Winckleman? She can't ever see you again. I didn't want her to mourn you for the rest of her life. And even if you outlive me by some freak chance, she knows too much. It's better that way. What else do you want? They could crown you president of the universe, and you still wouldn't be big enough. We're going to have our Reservation in the Bronx."

"Dream on, old man, but I didn't come here to fight. For God's sake, tell me more about AR. I can't get rid of my own addiction."

"What a dummy," David said. "I'm buying flame throwers, installing mini-tanks, and all you can think about is AR."

"I won't have any stories after you're gone. I'll be bereft. You've already stolen that picture of AR and Inez."

"What picture?"

"The one that was on Inez's bureau."

"I'll will it to you," David said. "I'll slide it into your coffin."

That sorcerer in the velvet slippers must have sniffed the bereavement in Isaac's eyes. He still had a touch of pity left in his bones. He could recall the short pants Isaac had worn on his first visit to the Ansonia. David didn't smell a child. He recognized an accomplice, a boy with murder in his blood . . . and a rival.

"I was disloyal to AR," he hissed with his own murderous intent. "I fucked his sweetheart, his Inez."

Isaac was stunned. "Before Arnold died?"

"Before and after," David said. And the old man could no longer tell if he was dreaming or not. He'd coveted Inez while AR was still alive, would glance at her cleavage like a sick dog. He was always sitting so close to her in Arnold's Pierce-Arrow, riding to Lindy's with her on leather cushions that were like a boudoir. And now he spat out all the details to Isaac Sidel. And this hoodlum mayor, who was ruining him day by day, stealing his lifeblood in the Bronx, stood there as if he were in a trance.

David couldn't mask his own bitterness. He'd had no life without Arnold's mistress. He stopped caring about the accounts. Her musk would drive him mad. Her skin had all the shine of Chinese paper. And when he snuggled up to her in the Pierce-Arrow, he almost wished there was no AR, no Lindy's delicatessen, but his logic was brutally wrong. Without that Broadway deli and its plate-glass windows, its greenish cloud of cigarette smoke, and its rambunctious waiters, he wouldn't have had to fetch Inez from the Ansonia, and had his own ambiguous romance in AR's limousine. It started when he was nine or ten. She'd sit with her knees in David's lap, hum a tune from the Follies, bite into her pearl cigarette holder, a gift from the Brain himself, Mr. Arnold Rothstein of Park Avenue and Lindy's— mail would come to him at the deli. The postmen adored him and would deliver letters with or without a stamp. Sometimes his name was scratched on the envelope, sometimes not. All it needed was the broadest stroke, a whiff of AR.

The Brain

Broadway

But it was Arnold's Little Brain who glanced at these letters first, and responded to them or threw their contents, with all their pathetic pleas, into the delicatessen's wastebasket. He wasn't running a Lonely Hearts Club for AR. The letters appalled him. Fathers trying to sell their own daughters to AR for the price of a sandwich; bachelors begging him for a loan to buy a silver kneecap or some other insane prosthetic device; mothers wanting to confide in him about the diminution of their sex life; old classmates and chums asking for an audience with the Brain . . .

Isaac groaned while David went through his inventory of notes to AR.

"Jesus, will ya get back to you and Inez in the Pierce-Arrow? I want some more meat on my potatoes."

"Meat and potatoes," the old man muttered and thrust the Big Guy right back into the world of Inez. She wouldn't tease a little boy, though she was blunt enough.

"You're Arnold's little spy," she said. "And I have to be nice to you. But I'm not the kind of girl who gives out sexual favors."

"I didn't ask for any," he said, his pockets stuffed with the Brain's markers and hundred-dollar bills.

"Shut up," she said, and with all the aplomb of a dancer who had floated down glass and silver steps in the Follies, she kissed the Little Brain, sucking half his head into the deliciously moist tunnel of her mouth.

"That's your future," she said. "Don't betray me, little man."

And David never did. He escorted her to the delicatessen twice a week. Arnold might have gotten suspicious had his own Little Brain suggested that Inez sit at his table one afternoon or evening more than that. Meanwhile, Arnold's markers began to mount.

He was a reckless gambler. He'd make a hundred grand on his various protection rackets and blow it on a bet about cockroaches climbing a wall. He'd *always* back the wrong roach.

Isaac clutched the old man's dilapidated sweater. "Stick to the story. *Inez.*"

And David had to laugh. "What a sucker you are. I could have stolen your pants while you were listening. Grow up. Be a mensch."

"I'll have enough time for that when I'm mothballed inside the Naval Observatory."

"You'll never get there, kid."

"I couldn't care less," Isaac told him. David wasn't a sorcerer—he was Scheherazade.

He had Inez in the Pierce-Arrow five fucking years. He mixed cocktails for her from the limo's little zinc bar, though she wouldn't even allow him one sip.

"Alcohol's bad business," she said. "It's not the right habit for a growing boy."

She would smile and brush the palm of her hand against his erection, like some clever item performing a magic trick. But she wasn't a clever item. Inez was always sincere, even when he grew into a boy of fourteen and she could have coupled with him in the back-seat. She would have galvanized David, had him forever in his debt.

"I really like you, Davey," she would purr, loud enough for the driver to hear. "Those brown eyes of yours really make me hot. I'm tingling like a potato on the fire. But you'd start to hate me, and I couldn't count on you after that."

And that's when he first wished AR's death. He couldn't become her darling, her favorite little man, while Arnold sat and breathed at his table. And so he grew a little careless. He paid less attention to AR's debts. And AR died because of a debt that David had noted in his books but had forgotten about.

Suddenly, his shoulders started to shake. He looked like a scarecrow in his sweater. He wasn't much of a sorcerer now. It was Isaac who had to wipe the tears from his eyes.

"Kiddo, I didn't need a Glock. I was his assassin."

"Come on," Isaac said. "He was marked for death."

"And I was the one who marked him."

"Okay, I'll cry for the son of a bitch, but what happened between you and Inez?"

And David told him how Inez had become his mistress after a fashion. She slept with no other man or boy but him.

"But there was always a monster in the bed, like a gigantic medieval sword."

"Arnold's ghost, you mean."

"No. Our guilt. I wooed her, and she must have been in love with me a little. But we felt like conspirators. Inez was nobody's fool."

She'd stare into his brown eyes after she came like a firecracker. And there was always that little smile. "Davey darling, I can't get over Arnold. We willed his demise."

He bought her flowers and little diamonds, took her on long rides in the Pierce-Arrow, which now belonged to him. She loved the panorama of Brighton Beach. She'd lived near the boardwalk when she started out at the Follies, a girl of fifteen, from Canton, Ohio.

"You Manhattanites mean nothing," she'd crow. "It's Midwesterners who made this town—me and Scott Fitzgerald."

Fitzgerald had long been gone from Manhattan by this time, had run to Hollywood without his mad wife. But David wouldn't contradict Inez. She began to shrink in his arms. Her skin no longer had the feel of Chinese paper. Most of her musk was gone. But he loved her more than ever. They'd become a pair of cripples. She wasn't even thirty-five when she died in David's arms, and she looked sixty. He buried her in Woodlawn, near the grave of Herman Melville, another New Yorker who had lived underground most of his life. But David's "underground" was in a limestone castle. And he'd kept his own lit candle to Inez and AR, in that little mausoleum on the thirteenth floor.

"You'd love to wreck my life, wouldn't you?" Isaac muttered. "Tell me where I can find Trudy Winckleman."

"Kiddo, I don't have room for another Inez in my heart. You'll never find her. And if you come here again, we'll hide you in the attic, and let the Ansonia's red rats have a field day. Have you ever seen a red rat? They can eat through steel. Imagine what they'll do to your blood and bones."

And David's own grim men tossed Isaac out of that stronghold on the seventeenth floor.

22

THE BIG GUY GOT NOWHERE with his snitches, or with the files on David Pearl at the NYPD. And so he went to his own mob source, Izzie Wasser, a.k.a. the melamed, who was the brains behind Manhattan's Mafia clans, even after he'd had a stroke. They met at Ratner's, a dairy restaurant near the Manhattan approach to the Williamsburg Bridge. It had long been downtown's answer to Lindy's, though it wasn't a delicatessen and didn't serve pastrami or roast beef. AR had never had his own table at Ratner's. But Isaac did.

He knew that Ratner's was dying, just as the old Lindy's had died and become a tourist's shrine at another location on Broadway. But he still had his table. Anyone could have walked in and shot out his lights, even as the nation's vice president–elect. But Isaac was "untouchable" in his very own mecca.

"Sonny," the melamed said, "I can't help you."

Isaac pleaded with him. "Iz, one lousy girl. Trudy Winckleman. Calls herself Inez. You have the best bloodhounds in the business."

"And what would my sources be worth if I ever betrayed the old man?"

"Jesus," Isaac mumbled, "what do you mean?"

"He's been our banker for sixty years. He's our landlord. He owns the building where we live—have some blintzes. You look like a ghost. We're proud of you. New York's next president, and you're one of us."

Isaac didn't contradict the melamed. "Then show me some respect. Tell me where Trudy Winckleman is."

"I could find her in ten minutes, but I won't. And you shouldn't rile that old man. He put you into the mayor's chair and never asked for a reward."

"Nobody put me in the mayor's chair. The Republicans didn't even field a candidate against me."

"Did you ever ask why? He financed them for a hundred years, just to keep out of the race."

Isaac got up from the table without touching his food. He kissed the melamed on the cheek and ran out of Ratner's. But he didn't get very far. Autograph hounds attached themselves to the Big Guy's coat. Jesus, he couldn't swat at them like flies. Soon he'd have to wear a fake nose in Manhattan—that was the limit. He wouldn't walk around with a schnozzola on the same mean streets where he'd been wandering for fifty years. Finally, he broke away from the hounds. His cuffs were torn. He'd have to buy a new shirt in the barrels of Orchard Street. But there were fewer and fewer barrels. Orchard Street was becoming a wonderland of boutiques.

The Big Guy kept imagining Trudy Winckleman's helmet of silver hair. Loath as he was to bring the FBI into the equation, he had to find her. No one but the Bull could pluck this second Inez from whatever hideout she was in. But he'd owe Bull Latham for life. He stood on Delancey Street and dialed the Bureau from a phone booth.

"Just tell him the Citizen needs a favor."

He had to wait with static in his ear.

"Sir," a voice said, "the director will be with you in sixty seconds."

"What the fuck is taking him so long?" he growled into the phone.

The Bull appeared in a Town Car. Isaac was disappointed. He'd
been dreaming of David Pearl's Pierce-Arrow. He climbed into the
backseat.

"You followed me to Ratner's, didn't you?"

"When you sit with the melamed, what do you expect, Mr.
President?"

"Then arrest me, you motherfucker."

The Bull started to laugh. "And if I did, we'd really have a crisis.
The country couldn't survive another election—we all depend on
you. Besides, the melamed is one of my best informants."

Isaac fell into a deep gloom. "The melamed belongs to the
Bureau? I'll never believe it. None of the clans could exist without
him. He's the real referee. He settles all the disputes. . . . Bull, you
ought to be president of the United States."

"Mister, I already am."

"That's grand," Isaac said. "And what about the wizard, David
Pearl, is he also registered with the Bureau?"

"Not a chance," said the Bull. "He could buy and sell the melamed.
But I'd watch out for that little number of his, the whore he kept on
his thirteenth floor. She ran a whole string of snatch houses in New
Orleans."

"I thought she was only the bookkeeper," Isaac grumbled.

"The bookkeeper-madam. Quite an inventory she had . . .with her
silver hair. She had every politician in Louisiana eating out of her lap.
Pearl must have paid a fortune to lure her from the Vieux Carré."

"She was destitute," Isaac said. "The old man let her stay on at the
Ansonia. He told me himself. She has some kids in Connecticut."

"That's where we're going—to Connecticut."

The Bull wanted to roar right across the Williamsburg Bridge
and invade Connecticut from Long Island Sound. The Bureau had
its own ferryboat waiting for Sidel.

"It will be like Washington crossing the Delaware. But you'll be
rescuing your lady love on this ride."

"Fuck the ferryboat," Isaac said. He wouldn't cross into Williams-burg; he always felt like a stranger in the wilds of Brooklyn, where no mayor, not even Isaac, had ever ruled. He had the Bull proceed up Manhattan's spine and spill into the wilds of East Harlem, which was much more familiar terrain. They skirted the ancient site of the Polo Grounds, like a wound in Isaac's heart. Yankee Stadium was just another castle to him. Isaac had *lived* at the Polo Grounds, had stolen through the gate countless times as a boy. He loved the New York Giants almost as much as he loved AR. He could become the next Methuselah, celebrate his thousandth birthday, and he still wouldn't recover from the Giants' betrayal of New York—they lit out for San Francisco like a pack of greedy dogs. The bastards took Willie Mays, who had to stop playing stickball in the streets of Har-lem. He was never the Say Hey Kid in San Francisco, just another ballplayer with a sweet bat and glove . . . and without the empty plains of the Polo Grounds.

Isaac grieved. He wouldn't let Bull Latham onto the Cross Bronx. "I'll become a dynamiter, Bull, I swear. I'll blow it all up."

"Why bother? They'll build another one."

"I don't care, as long as Robert Moses writhes in his grave."

The ride started to rankle Isaac, as they went through neighbor-hoods that Moses had ripped right from the ground. They were in the middle of a wasteland, with rubble, rude grass, and concrete storage bins, where the Bronx had once had its Strivers' Row—East Tremont, enclave of the lower middle class. The Big Guy had been in love with a Tremont beauty. He rode the Third Avenue El half the night to see his Rosalind. But her father didn't trust a boy with woolly ears. Isaac had to sneak her into the Loew's Paradise. That was his only boudoir. They kissed for three hours under the Para-dise's "atmospheric" sky—a constellation of clouds and brutal, blink-ing stars. But she'd sworn herself to a midshipman in the navy and wouldn't let Isaac near her bloomers. That must have been around '47, when Isaac was still a young gallant from the Lower East Side.

She sent him a fan letter a few years ago, swore she had never forgotten their trysts under the stars. She was now a widow of fifty-five, as handsome as ever. But Isaac didn't have the heart to see her. It would have ruined his memory of Rosalind. . . .

They passed block after block of burnt brick carcasses.

"This is where the Pentagon will build its Reservation, isn't it, Bull?"

"Mr. President, it's a soldier's paradise. The military will survive most administrations. The White House has a bunch of screaming children. But the generals don't have to scream. I'd be a liar if I told you I wasn't betting on them."

"But the mayor of New York watches over real estate. It's his barn. I could have shut down Yankee Stadium even after the strike was over. And it's too bad that the Giants disappeared before my watch. I would have sued the shit out of them. They'd never have gotten past the Harlem River."

"Or else they could have learned to swim. But it doesn't matter, Mr. President. Your town will soon have another mayor."

Isaac closed his eyes as they bumped onto the New England Thruway. He couldn't say why, but he dreaded meeting Trudy Winckleman in Connecticut. Perhaps he could only love her as a museum piece. He was a great big romantic bear. But it wasn't in the realm of romance. Something else bothered the Big Guy. His intuition had abandoned him beyond the borders of the Bronx. He was headed for heartbreak.

23

S HE LIVED IN A MODEST ranch house in the woods near Waterbury. It looked as if it had been built out of tarpaper and tack
and might not survive the next hurricane. He didn't ask the
Bull to come inside with him. But he cursed himself. He should
have brought her flowers or some book, like *Anna Karenina*. His
biggest sorcerers at City Hall had told him there would be no books
in another ten thousand years. Paper would turn to dust, with all
the bricks, glass, and concrete. The Ansonia itself would disappear.
Isaac didn't give a damn. But he would have been lonely without his
favorite characters.

He'd only had one semester at Columbia College. He still wept
over Anna and that rascal, Richard III. He, too, would have given
his kingdom for a horse. And if he'd ever had Richard's gifts, he
might have wooed his silver-haired lady with nothing but words.
His mind was broken, and he couldn't remember how many children Karenina had—one with her snake of a husband and another
with her weak-willed adorer, Count Vronsky? And how would Isaac

deal with Inez's own kids? Was he as weak as that adorer? Or would he ride into the plains with Inez, renounce his own vice presidency?

He knocked on her door. There were no hobbyhorses on the lawn, no jungle gyms, not a single sign of Inez's brats. She still had that silver helmet of hers. But her eyes had gone dead at the first sight of Sidel. He wanted to leap into the woods and live with all the wild deer.

"Come inside," she said. He had to follow her like a wayward pilgrim. They landed in the kitchen. A man was sitting at the table. He wore a holster without a gun. He could have been a lost troubadour, or a defeated wolf, with stubble on his chin and a listless, cruel look. He was much younger than Isaac. That's what hurt. She introduced him as her husband, Arno. He nursed the same green bottle as the Bull, drinking Jameson whiskey in the middle of the afternoon.

"Trudy," Isaac said, "I didn't mean . . . "

And now her eyes lit with a touch of fever, like those stars in the ceiling of the Loew's Paradise.

"Darling, I'm still Inez," she told him. "And Arno can't stay. He has chores to do."

This troubadour left the kitchen without a word. And then Inez started to weep. Her shoulders shook. She turned away from Isaac. "Don't look at me. I'm a witch whenever I cry. My face puffs out . . . and my hair starts to sizzle. Can you imagine that? A mama whose own head is a fire hazard."

He didn't know what do. He was another lost troubadour. He wanted to hold her in his arms, swallow up whatever fears she had, like arrows in the chest.

"You weren't supposed to come here," she said. "That was the deal. David said you would never find me."

"But I did find you."

Suddenly she started to cackle. And she could have been the witch of Connecticut. And then her face softened again. She almost smiled.

"My poor little darling, how dumb can you be? You weren't supposed to find your Inez. David closed every resource, locked you out of my life."

She was wearing a sweater, as old and worn as David's. And then he realized that it was one of David's relics. *Another museum piece.* And the Big Guy was brutally jealous. Part of the sleeve had begun to unravel, and Isaac touched the threads.

"That old man doesn't own the world," Isaac muttered.

"But he owns me. . . . Darling, don't you get it? I'm his captive. He has my little son and my daughter."

"But you said they were at boarding school—in Connecticut."

"And who boards them? *David Pearl.* They live in his house, with his housekeeper, his bodyguards. I have to beg each time I want to see them. . . . Isaac, I'm scared. Sometimes I blank out, forget their faces, their names."

"But you have a husband."

Her hands trembled, and her whole body began to heave, until her silver helmet whipped about in its own wind. And then it all stopped.

"*Husband*, that's what I call him. Arno is one of David's gunmen. He watches over me."

"A gunman without a gun."

"Arno doesn't need a gun," she insisted. "The holster is just for show. The whole place is surrounded. Why, why did you come here?"

"I love you," Isaac said without the least hesitation.

"Damn you, I'm just a trick. David hired me to worm my way into your heart. And he knew I'd fall for an adorable idiot like you. That's why he kept his insurance—my kids."

"But I'll rescue them," Isaac said.

"Keep away. You'll get them killed. . . . Darling, you can't even rescue yourself."

Isaac looked deep into the puzzle of her eyes. "But I have Bull Latham outside. And he has the full firepower of the FBI."

And now the witch of Connecticut looked like a sad little waif.

"Isaac, he's the one who led you into this trap. He's David Pearl's best bounty hunter."

"Come on," Isaac said. "Not even David can bribe the whole Bureau."

"David doesn't have to do a thing when he has the president on his side."

"But how can Cottonwood help him?"

She put her hands over her eyes and started to shake again. "Stop talking," she said. "I'm the only one who can get you out of here alive—not your Glock, not Bull Latham. . . . What is it you want? To sleep with Inez one last time? Isaac, I'm nothing but a dream inside your head, a ghost who walked out of a museum."

The Big Guy was terribly aroused. He couldn't help himself—pain had become his aphrodisiac, pain woke him out of his slumber, pain and his own hunger for Inez. She shucked off her sweater and her skirt. Her lovely arms were dappled with goose bumps. He didn't have to reconnoiter in the bedroom. Isaac wouldn't have known where it was.

He made love to Inez on the flat of the table. And for the first time in his life, Isaac felt safe, wondrously safe, while he could hold onto her dappled flesh.

He couldn't even say what pleasure he had given Inez. His spittle mingled with hers while they were on that tabletop. Her goose bumps disappeared. She got dressed.

And then she called for Arno. That demented wolf returned with his cruel mouth. He was smiling at Isaac. He took a pouch of Bugler's from his pocket and rolled a cigarette for himself and Inez. He couldn't have been a local hood. Bugler wasn't cultivated in Manhattan or the Bronx. Arno must have come from West Texas or the Alamo. Isaac wondered if he'd ever seen this killer in the cattlemen's bar at Menger's. Meanwhile, Inez signaled with the palm of her hand that he should stay where he was and not interfere in her business.

"Arno," she said with the Bugler in her mouth. "You'll take him home—in one piece."

"And ef I don't?" he said in a West Texas drawl.

"Then Isaac is gonna move in with me."

"Fat chance, Miz Inez. He might not breathe another ten minutes. You'll be the widuh lady before you're a bride."

And he started to titter. Inez slapped his face. He was flooded with anger, but he wouldn't hit her back.

"If you hurt him, Arno, you know what will happen next."

"Yes'um. Mr. David's gonna give me a big fat reward."

"And after that? I'll crawl into your bedroom while you're fast asleep, and I'll cut your prick off with the sharpest knife I can find."

Arno's eyes began to dart inside his skull. Then he laughed. "Miz Inez, you shouldn't give your plans away. I'm liable to hurt ya real bad."

"And what will Mr. David think when he discovers your own paw prints on my arm? You'll escort Mr. Isaac home, and God help you if anything happens to him."

She wouldn't even let Isaac say good-bye in front of Arno. She shoved him out the door with just a little bit of a caress. Inez didn't even wait there. She went back inside and shut the door. The sound broke into the night like a melancholy whisper. Isaac couldn't see much. But he knew that Bull Latham wasn't out there. Bull had abandoned him.

David's lieutenants, wild little men, wearing medieval vests they must have swiped or borrowed from the NYPD, drove him out of Connecticut in some crazy vintage car with armored windows and maroon-colored seats. With all his gloom, it took him a whole hour to realize that it was David's Pierce-Arrow, inherited from AR himself. He could imagine the first Inez, the real one, on these cushions with David . . . and AR. But even that memory couldn't melt his gloom. His melancholy grew as they arrived at the front gate of Gracie Mansion.

The guards were curious, but they let him through. He climbed out of the Pierce-Arrow and trudged across the gravel. Marianna was waiting for him at the front door, like the mayor's own little wife. She must have grown an inch in the last couple of days. Her shoulders seemed to burst. She had as much vitality as a mountain lion.

"Uncle Isaac, where have you been? We were worried to death."

The Big Guy wove around Marianna and went inside.

PART SIX

24

SHE'D GROWN UP IN A bagnio, the best in New Orleans. Her favorite "aunt" was a whore with a head of silver hair. Auntie looked after her, made sure none of the customers sniffed her underpants. Some of the other girls had been cruel. But Auntie protected her in this constant tug-of-war. And after a while, Auntie became manager of the Blond Moon, its very own madam, and she managed other bagnios for the mob. She sent her little orphan to school, but it was a waste of time. Trudy had become the bagnio's bookkeeper. She could toss off figures on her fingertips, add magnificent sums in her head. She never cheated the girls who had been unkind to her. And she always prepared the correct "cut" for mobsters and members of the Orleans Parish police—there wasn't much of a difference between them.

She fell in love with a crooked cop, as handsome as a blue-eyed sailor. But he had one wife in the Garden District and another in Algiers. Trudy didn't care. She fed off his blue eyes. She had two kids with this cop. She raised her kids right in the bagnio, where her lovely cop could sleep when he wasn't with his other wives. He gave Trudy a silver ring and told her not to wear it. The other girls called him Jew Boy, because he didn't like hard liquor and he never beat any of his wives. But he must have been part of the wrong patrol. He was shot in the head by another member of the Parish police. The cops called it the result of a drunken brawl, but her Jew Boy never drank.

No one was ever prosecuted. Other cops knocked on her door, said they wanted her to become their little mama. She'd cackle at them and wield a kitchen knife. They called her a fruitcake and found new mamas for themselves, ones who were a bit more docile and wouldn't mind the protection they could offer. But she managed to survive under Auntie's wing. It was Auntie who had pulled her right out of the public orphanage with the help of mobsters who ran the Parish. Auntie had seen "Little Miss Sad Eyes" washing clothes and decided that she would fit into the landscape of the Blond Moon. It was like picking a puppy she didn't have to pay for.

The girl had been saddled with a preposterous name—Marissa Dawn. No one could find her birth certificate, but that's what she was called at the orphanage. Auntie didn't dare use it at the Blond Moon. It was a whore's moniker. And it might give her customers ideas. They were always looking to pierce some child's cherry. And so Auntie shielded her with her own name. And this orphan with the big brown eyes would become Little Trudy Winckleman. . . .

She worked like a dog, and was the bookkeeper of Auntie's bagnios by the time she was fifteen. She was a mother before she was twenty. She was twenty-six when Auntie died. Now she herself had to manage the bagnios. And now she had a scalp of silver hair. The children went to private schools and lived with her in the Quarter. Daniel and Darl. All the new mamas at the Blond Moon would turn up their noses and tell her that *Darl* wasn't much of a name.

"It's short for Darling," she'd shout and silence those mamas. But she was still ashamed. She shouldn't have kept her children in a bagnio, but she worked night and day, and where else could she keep them? Darl smoldered a lot. She was as tall as any mama at the Blond Moon, and she was only ten.

There were brutal fights between the old Creole gangs and the gangs of black New Orleans. The white overlords were dying out. The cops harassed her. And she didn't like how they looked at Darl, following her home from school, offering to give her a ride.

They're after my little girl's cherry, Trudy sang inside her head. She ran out of New Orleans with Daniel and Darl. She didn't have much cash in her pockets. And she had to leave the bagnios' strongbox behind, else the crime lords would insist she had stolen from them and might harm her babies. She landed in another "Parish," the isle of Manhattan, and found a sublet at a building that could have been part of its own French Quarter—it had turrets and gargoyles that reminded her of bearded little devils right out of Mardi Gras. But she couldn't pay the rent. Suddenly, she had a rescuer.

She wouldn't have accepted *anything* from him, but he was kind to Daniel, and he didn't steal looks at Trudy or her little girl. She'd knocked on his door and discovered a hobo in velvet slippers, a hobo who was also a billionaire. And he startled her.

"I always wanted to meet Marissa Dawn."

How could he have known her name at the orphanage? Had he been friendly with the crime lords of Orleans Parish? Would the hobo collect on their debt? Would he steal Darl from her? It was even more mysterious than that. He'd been one of the Blond Moon's secret owners, had been familiar with her Auntie. He was a landlord who had never sold a single property, he said. And he had a proposition for her.

"The bosses will find you, and they'll break your bones. But I can hide you, Miss Marissa Winckleman Dawn, hide you and your children."

They weren't safe at the Ansonia, he said. But he'd enroll them at a school in Connecticut, the best that money could buy, and she could visit the children, have her own pied-à-terre, when she wasn't working for him. But she had to decide in half a minute. He introduced himself as David Pearl, the protégé and former partner of Arnold Rothstein, Manhattan's first king of crime. He told her all about Inez, the Ziegfeld Follies girl Rothstein had adored, and how David had also adored her. He'd never leased out Inez's old apartment on the thirteenth floor. . . .

And so she became Inez. It was an ideal way of submerging her identity. The crime lords of Orleans Parish would never find her now. And suppose she was the curator of an eccentric museum? This old man was in love with a creature who had died fifty years ago, and he never asked her to talk or dress like his own personal phantom. She played out her part, lived in that museum, but he went too far. He threw her at this crazy cop, Isaac Sidel, who happened to be mayor and vice president–elect.

"You don't have to romance him," David said. "Just drive him out of his mind."

She smiled at this potentate in the velvet slippers. "The way Inez did to Rothstein . . . and you?"

"Yeah, yeah. But Sidel doesn't have much of a future. He'll be dead within a month. Distract him, and there'll be a bonus for you and the kids."

And that's what crippled her, having to entice a mayor with a death sentence hanging over his woolly ears. He was another Jew Boy, another cop, but he didn't have washboard abdominals and blue eyes. And he wasn't the father of her two babies. But something stirred in her, like a strange twist in her loins. He *felt* like the father of her children, as if he could love them with a lunatic devotion without having met either one. That was her dilemma. She wanted to introduce this cop to Daniel and Darl, and yet it would compromise their cover and might be dangerous for them. And while she deliberated, she fell in love with the big, burly bear.

She'd slept with no other man since her blue-eyed cop, had wanted no other man, and here was Isaac Sidel. He worshiped Arnold Rothstein, worshiped the museum, and might have worshiped her as its curator, but he never once confused her with Rothstein's Inez. And she kept thinking to herself, *Will the idiot live long enough to meet Daniel or Darl?* And she realized she didn't want him to die.

But she couldn't become his accomplice. The old man would turn into an ogre, tear her babies to shreds. And so she tried to rid herself of Isaac Sidel. But the old man must have sensed her ambivalence. His gunmen pulled her right out of the Ansonia and hid her in Connecticut. She thought she was safe from Sidel. But the dummy appeared like her own forlorn knight when Daniel and Darl's existence was at stake. And the chief of all the gunmen, a psycho called Arno, whom she had to placate with an occasional kiss, and who was known as her "husband" among those other maniacs, chortled at the sight of Sidel.

"Ef'n it ain't the boogeyman?"

And she had to become *his* savior now. She had to frighten the psychopath, this gunman without a gun, and soothe him at the same time, or Sidel would never have escaped. Ah, it was her best performance as Inez. And she didn't even have to wiggle her tush. She hadn't been the bookkeeper to an arcade of whores for nothing. She managed to twist the wires in Arno's head, to shock him into letting Sidel go free.

But she couldn't even pull on the dummy's ears and give him a genuine kiss in front of that psychopath, or Arno would have succumbed to a jealous rage. But she panicked once Sidel was gone, had a sadness she might not survive. She missed his bearish ways. And when Arno came near her, she lashed at him.

"Smoke your Buglers, or I'll make you strangle on your own tobacco."

"Ef you ain't nice, Miz Inez, I'll hurt your chilrun, I swear I will."

He shouldn't have threatened her like that; she imagined Daniel and Darl with broken faces and eyeless eyes, and she lunged at him. And that's when the old man came through the door in his slippers, with her *chilrun*. Daniel seemed utterly self-sufficient, as if he were a character in his own dream and was having a discussion with himself. He wasn't much older than nine, but he could survive better than his sister. She'd given him the old, tattered bear she'd had at the orphanage, an animal without eyes or a name, and he carried it everywhere. But Darl didn't have the same kind of talisman. Darl was a sufferer, like Marissa Winckleman Dawn. Her eyes were as sad as Sidel's.

"Mother," she said with her practiced imperial tone, "how long will we have to live alone? I adore Daniel, but a nine-year-old boy can't be my only companion. I'll wither away."

She must have seen the whores in front of their mirrors, even when she was a child. It was their imperiousness she had copied.

"Baby," Inez said, "I'm doing whatever I can."

"But that isn't enough, is it, Mr. David?"

"Ah," the old man said, "we'll see, we'll see."

And he turned on his own gunman. "Arno, you let that Isaac walk away?"

The gunman began to whimper. "It's her fault, Mr. David. The bitch threatened me."

David slapped him with his own delicate fingers, and that slap must have cost him more than it did the gunman without a gun.

"Arno, if you ever disparage a mother in front of her children again, I'll have you executed."

"I'm sorry, Mr. David," the gunman said. And he was so nervous that he began to make a sucking sound. David wanted to talk to Inez in private, but Darl clung to her, dug into Inez with her own sharp hip. Inez didn't mind. It was like being kissed by a pet shark.

"It's an emergency," the old man said. "It's like walking through a street of trained crocodiles. And I'm stuck in the middle."

"But, Mr. David," Darl said, "there are no crocodiles in Connecticut."

"Yes there are, if you look hard enough."

And he turned to Inez. "You'll have to say good-bye to the kids. If Isaac finds them, I'm all out of ammunition. He'll ease up on his crocodiles while I have them . . . and you. I might even survive the century."

She could have scratched his eyes out and raced from this ranch house in the middle of nowhere—her *husband* would have been in shock for half an hour. She pitied Arno and his stinking tobacco. But where could she go? The crime lords would have found her and sold her back into slavery. And she'd have to live above the Blond Moon with Daniel and Darl. Sooner or later, her own daughter would have to perform tricks.

"David, when will I see them again?"

"That depends on Sidel. I'll be safe once he drops dead."

But she couldn't wish the death of her own big bear, not even for her children's sake. So difficult as it was, she had to separate herself from Darl.

"Baby," she whispered, "go with the bad man."

And she knew that Darl would rebel, would hurl herself away from Inez in her anger.

"Mr. David isn't bad, Mother. You are."

And now Daniel started to cry. His sister had confused him, and Daniel was plucked out of his own comfortable dream. He clutched his eyeless bear.

"Mommy, would you send us away with a bad man?"

"Not unless that bad man could save you, darling."

And now David Pearl began to pick at the patches of his sweater like a raw wound.

"I'm touched," he said. "I'm melting away with tears. But we have no more time to kill. And if Connecticut gets into my blood, I'm a goner."

The children went with him, vanished from the house. She didn't even ask for a kiss. If she had sniffed Daniel's hair, caught herself in his own sweet sweat, she wouldn't have had the heart to relinquish him. And now she'd have a little eternity with Arno and the other gunmen. And she could start plotting her escape, even if she had nowhere else to go, and knew her plots would unravel into nothing, just like the old man's sweater.

She began singing to herself.

Sidel will save them, Sidel will save them.

But then she recalled that Sidel had never met Darl, had never seen Daniel's face. She withdrew into her own melancholy, and the gunmen decided that it was best to leave the bitch alone.

PART SEVEN

25

SAAC SURVIVED THE JANUARY BLUES. Both houses of Congress convened and certified the election. Isaac and J. Michael were no longer in limbo. The nation had an *official* president-elect. Michael couldn't be tampered with. No indictment could get rid of him now. The Democratic National Committee began to crow. Ramona Dazzle had picked out her dress for the inauguration balls, designed by Givenchy. She commuted between Washington and Paris for the fittings. Like Clarice Storm, she began to live on the Concorde. But the papers couldn't have cared less about either of them.

The Little First Lady was seen on the cover of *Vogue* in a gown she had fashioned for herself at Isaac's mansion. The inaugural parade was already mapped out. Isaac would sit with the Little First Lady in the presidential procession. She alone would be Isaac's escort. She had to have her own press secretary and her own office at Gracie Mansion. She hardly had time for school. Her press secretary was that star clerk, Amanda Wilde. Isaac felt that he had a spy in his own house. But he couldn't fire Amanda. It would have broken the Little First Lady's heart.

His face went black around the star clerk. He would capture her in the hallway, on a remote landing. He felt as deformed as Richard III, and just as cunning in his own dark cloud.

"I'll strangle you," he said. "No one will weep for you, not even Marianna. I'll bury you in the garden with my own bare hands. What is David plotting? You were his secretary."

"And his accountant," Miranda muttered. "I kept his books. But I haven't betrayed you—or Marianna. I helped her with the inaugural gown. I picked out the colors."

"You're still a star clerk . . . and David's own Cassandra. What is that wizard betting on? It doesn't matter now if Michael falls or doesn't fall. I'll inherit his mantle. And I'll make war on that old man."

"He might welcome a war from you," Miranda said. "But he doesn't trust Michael. He never did. Michael is much too greedy."

He left her there on the landing, like a lonesome dove. And he had a terrible wound in his own gut as he recalled Trudy Winckleman's words. *David doesn't have to do a thing when he has the president on his side.* Dummy that he was, a son of the Loew's Paradise, with a movie palace's stars still in his skull, he should have realized that she wasn't talking about Cottonwood. She was talking about David's *other* partner, Michael Storm, the guy who would sacrifice his own fucking daughter to the billions he might make in the Bronx. Isaac would have to destroy Sidereal once and for all. But none of the city's own lawyers would assist him in the wreckage.

"Your Honor, we have no case."

Sidereal was wrapped in its own enigma. Besides, he might hurt Marianna, who was one of Sidereal's officers, together with Michael and Clarice. The city's lawyers explained everything to him. Michael couldn't sit on Sidereal once he wore the president's crown. He'd have to relinquish his holdings in Sidereal and put all his assets into a blind trust. *There's the rub.* He'd sell out to the wizard and remain a silent partner. And he'd really cash in once the wild lands and burnt terraces of the Bronx became the biggest fort in the USA.

He couldn't even run to Ramona Dazzle; she was much too involved with Givenchy to meet with the vice president–elect. Isaac's own stock had fallen once Congress confirmed Michael as the country's next king. Tim Seligman was blunt with him.

"Isaac, you should have gotten rid of Michael when you had the chance. America can't have more than one king at a time. It's much too confusing."

The DNC had stopped answering his calls. It was ensconced with Michael at the Waldorf. That's how it was with presidential politics. The vice president was always a pariah. He would have to sulk within the walls of his own mansion at the Naval Observatory. Minutes from the White House, on a lovely hill near Rock Creek, Isaac's new dwelling was an eternity away from the White House. He would have his own office in the West Wing, with his own staff, but Isaac knew that his staff and Michael's would never meet. He'd have to take advantage of his last few moments as mayor of Manhattan and the Bronx.

He'd never been so ostracized, so alone. He couldn't rely on anyone but an invalid, his son-in-law, Joey, who'd been knocked on the head. But Joey had disappeared from his hospital room. And just as Isaac began to brood, his son-in-law found him. Barbarossa had a whole racial salad in his bones. He was descended from the Pierced Noses, or Nez Percé, an Indian tribe known for its chivalry—it never harmed a single prisoner. Barbarossa also had a pinch of African blood in his veins. Every single cop at the NYPD was afraid of Vietnam Joe.

"Joey," Isaac said, "we have to go to the guns."

"Dad, we have no guns."

"But they're gonna steal the Bronx from us and turn it into some huge tent for the military. It has its own landlord—David Pearl."

"Dad, who the fuck is he?"

"Arnold Rothstein's ghost."

Isaac groaned as he said it. AR wouldn't have plundered an entire borough, wouldn't have sent an army of arsonists into the streets. And AR had protected *his* Inez, and wouldn't have banished her to Connecticut.

"And this ghost has gone to his own gunsels. They've been rounding up people left in the dunes and hurling them into huts on the far side of the Bronx River."

"Dad, the Bronx doesn't have a *real* river—it's just a stream to piss in. But I have a solution. Rondo Raines."

Raines presided at the Abyssinian Baptist Church on Webster Avenue—a rogue minister who had fought firebugs and federal marshals from the smoldering ruins of his church. Rondo was making his own last stand in the Bronx. He'd been in and out of Riker's during the past six months. But Isaac had never bothered to learn Rondo's pedigree.

He hadn't always been the minister of a black church in the Bronx. He was once a marine chaplain in Nam who supplied dope to his "parishioners." The dope kept these men sane *and* alive. He was also the one and only black Crusader in Nam. He'd grown up in Colorado County, Texas, as the thirteenth son of a sharecropper. His folks had tilled the same soil for generations, had been the grandsons of slaves. He'd attended a black seminary in East Texas and had gone right from the seminary to Saigon. He'd moved to the Bronx after the war as minister of a church in the Bronx that no one else wanted. Its earlier ministers had met with some fatality after six months or so. He was the longest-surviving minister that the church on Webster had ever had.

It took half the day for Joey and Isaac to find him. Rondo Raines had become the Bronx's vanishing Zapata—he ran from dune to dune, helping people hide from David's bloodhounds and taking a stand whenever he could. Joe had tracked him to the church's bombed-out basement. He wasn't wearing any clerical garb. He couldn't travel very far in a maroon robe. He wore a tattered military tunic and a pair of Old Gringo boots with hammered silver down its sides. He wasn't very tall. He was a slight, delicate man with a goatee.

UNDER THE EYE OF GOD

He was pleased as the devil to see Joe, but he eyed the mayor and vice president–elect with suspicion.

"Joey, I forgive you for your father-in-law, but why did you have to bring such a godless man into the House of the Lord?"

"He wants to help you," Barbarossa said.

"Help me? Politicians only help themselves."

Barbarossa muttered something, but Isaac interrupted him.

"Jesus, Joey, will you let me get in a word?"

Rondo rose up from the floor of the basement and walloped Isaac on the jaw with one knuckle. The Big Guy landed on his ass, in the dust of this disemboweled church. Surely he could trust a man who socked him like that.

"Sidel, if you ever dishonor the Lord's Only Son again, I'll give you a hernia inside your head."

"Joey," Isaac sang, "who is this guy? I love him."

"Mr. Mayor, I'd be much happier if you loved me a little less."

And Isaac told him his plan—to catch David Pearl's private sheriffs in the badlands of the Bronx and shoot the shit out of them.

Rondo Raines was bewildered. "And you can protect me from the law? Sidel, you are the law."

"Not when I'm in the Bronx," Isaac said. "Then I'm the meanest motherfucker around."

"Hey, dog, what if I don't believe you? I start shootin', I go right to jail."

"And I'll sit in the same cell with you," Isaac said. "Me and Joe."

"But they're firebugs. They got fuckin' flamethrowers."

"Then we'll have to put out their flames."

■ ■ ■

DAVID'S SHERIFFS ARRIVED IN THE dunes in their own armored car. They'd come to chase out the inhabitants of the last building that stood on Hoe Avenue and 172nd. It was a six-story tenement of burnished brick that still housed the Nuyoricans of Southern Boulevard and the South Bronx. It was a neighborhood that had no protection, not even from dope dealers. These were the last cave dwellers in the Bronx. The cops wouldn't patrol streets of rubble; there was neither electricity nor gas, and you couldn't hear the sound of a single telephone.

Still, the sheriffs arrived in the middle of the night with their flamethrowers and their little packets of cash. They called up to the windows.

"Muchachos, we don't mean any harm. We have a cash incentive. Three hundred dollars and a new home with a fridge that spits out ice. We'll give you half a minute to decide."

A voice sang to them from a certain window. "Hey, dog, I'll be right down."

These sheriffs didn't like the sound of it. They'd dealt with Rondo Raines before, but he'd never serenaded them from a window. It was always hit-and-run with Rondo Raines.

He waltzed right out of the building in his Old Gringo boots. He didn't seem to have his pair of sawed-off shotguns that he carried around like pirate pistols. They meant to murder him. And they even saw that wacko Sidel, who was in love with Mr. David's whore. Well, they'd murder him, too. And then Barbarossa appeared on their blind side. Vietnam Joe. And they didn't even have a chance to turn him into a tar baby with their flamethrower. It was these maniacs who shot first—didn't ask for a truce. It wasn't fair. There'd never been the least element of danger in their rides into the Bronx.

Rondo pulled pirate pistols out of his sleeves. But it wasn't like a gunfight in the Wild West where bullets went astray, pistols exploded, and it was hard as hell to shoot a man. This was the Wild, Wild East. And when the dust cleared, all five sheriffs lay dead, slumped against the cracked windows of their armored car.

26

ISAAC HELD A PRESS CONFERENCE right in the dunes, at the very scene of the crime. Not a hair had been touched. Reporters arrived from all over the planet. How many vice president–elects had ever been involved in a firefight? The media dubbed it *O.K. Corral in the Bronx*. The French and Germans had their own television crews. The Japanese had a little army of cameramen. All the networks were there.

Isaac stood near Barbarossa and Rondo Raines and held up the flamethrower. "These were murderers," he said. "As brutal as they come. They meant to burn up the building and us with it. Folks, we had to defend ourselves."

The coronation was a week away, and no one talked of Michael and Clarice, or cared if she brought her own bodyguard, Bernardo, into the White House. Even the *Inquirer* wasn't interested in Bernardo Dublin. It was all Isaac Sidel. Democratic voters began to grumble that their ticket was topsy-turvy. Sidel had the gravitas, not J. Michael Storm. And Sidel had the Glock.

Suddenly, Ramona Dazzle wasn't so interested in her inauguration gown. She wanted to sit down with Sidel. He ducked her and the DNC. He would meet with no one but his son-in-law and that rogue minister from the dunes of the Bronx. Reporters were eager to learn what role Rondo Raines would have on Isaac's team.

"I have no team," Isaac said. "Rondo is my whittle mate."

Reporters scratched their heads. "Whittle mate?"

"Yeah, dog, we'll sit under a tree at the Naval Observatory and whittle wooden ducks. What else does a vice president have to do?"

Finally, it was his own daughter, Marilyn, who had to ride right under the radar and shake him out of his stubborn sleep.

"Father dear, you'll have to name a chief of staff."

"What for?" he growled

She was the only one who could cuff him on the ear and get away with it.

"Because that's what vice presidents do while they're whittling wooden ducks. They have a chief of staff."

There was only one possible candidate, a reclusive film teacher at the New School, where Marilyn had registered for an occasional course. Her name was Brenda Brown. She'd been chief of production at Paramount Pictures before she was twenty-five and was considered the girl wonder of Hollywood. She'd had a liaison with one of Paramount's star actresses, but the actress shot herself in Brenda's Malibu mansion, after a lover's quarrel, and Brenda quickly fell from grace. She was locked out of her office at Paramount. Agents wouldn't answer her calls. She fled her own mansion and moved to a house in Greenwich Village where Edna St. Vincent Millay had once lived.

A little before the election, Isaac had accidentally bumped into her while he was giving a lecture at the New School. She was a short, dumpy woman who wouldn't wear makeup; she had long eyelashes and was beautiful in spite of her fleshy face. She'd spent half an hour telling him what a lousy mayor he was. Isaac adored her critique. She wouldn't pander to the Big Guy.

"Mr. Mayor," she had told him, "think of the city as one colossal film production company. And how can you run it if you can't delegate power? You're marvelous for publicity—the mayor with a gun. But you can't Glock every problem out of existence."

Brenda *and* Marilyn knew how to bust his balls. But the Big Guy had a problem. He might fancy himself as Richard III, who had the will to woo queens and princes, but he wasn't sure whether he could woo Brenda out of her hermit's life. He met with her at Gracie and started to stutter.

He wanted to tell her about the Queen Anne chairs at 1 Naval Observatory Circle, how she would have to take charge of the furnishings and the staff.

"I'm not into decor," she said. "And that's the least of your problems. But you have to decide what to do with Michael. When should we get rid of him? After the inauguration—or before? But he has to go. We can't let a prick like that have so much power. Americans will suffer from his mistakes . . . and his greed."

But Isaac stalled, couldn't seem to make up his mind. And then Michael began to reveal the heart of his new administration. The president-elect wanted a "unity cabinet." Sumner Mars would remain as secretary of defense. The new man at Treasury was a heartless son of a bitch who'd had dealings with Sidereal. A dark pulse beat above Isaac's left eye. Brenda worried that her boss was having a stroke. Isaac did see blood. He looked like a madman in this own mirror.

"We have to get rid of Michael right away."

"Listen, dog," Rondo said. "We can't use a flamethrower on him. It's illegal."

But Brenda understood all the mental machinery of her new boss. She went into her files and found the name of a PI who had worked for her at Paramount. The PI was considered a miracle man. Within two days, a story broke on all the wire services that J. Michael Storm, president-elect, had a love child. The mother of the child produced scabrous photos of J. and herself. She appeared on a local TV show in Denver—the narrative bounced from network to network. Ramona Dazzle and the DNC couldn't even shield Michael. It was a little too late for damage control. The DNC called her a harlot who had taken advantage of the president-elect right before his coronation ball, but he began to look more and more like a serial seducer and a heartless man. It was the Little First Lady who delivered the coup de grâce. "I'd love to say hello to my half brother," she purred in front of the cameras. She must have known what folly it would have been to have her dad in the White House. She had the makings of a killer politician *and* a movie star.

Michael held on for two days, and then he had to run for the hills. Ninety percent of the populace declared that he wasn't fit to be president. He didn't even hold a press conference. He scribbled a letter of resignation to the DNC. Clarice had a nervous breakdown and called Marianna a witch. Tim Seligman and Ramona Dazzle hiked up to Gracie Mansion. Their faces had a bitter white color as they saw their own leverage slip.

"We're not crazy about Brenda Brown," Tim said. "She's much too controversial. She'll hurt the Democrats."

"Well, dog," Isaac said, "then tell me who should be my chief of staff?"

"Ramona. She's a perfect fit. She can fend off the Republicans when they try to attack."

"Timmy," Isaac said, "you're a sweetheart."

He left them stranded at Gracie and rode up to the badlands with Rondo and Brenda Brown. He stood in the rubble on Hoe Avenue, next to the building that had nearly burnt down. He waited for fifteen minutes, while the reporters and camera crews began to appear in the wind and dust. He stared into the merciless eye of each camera, the Glock sticking out of his pants. He was mayor and sheriff and the new president-elect.

"Ladies and gentlemen," he said, "these streets are mine, and whoever would steal them from me will pay a bitter price. But I'm still not satisfied. I've seen some of the same streets in Texas, in Illinois, in South Carolina, the same hunger, the same sad eyes, and I mean to do something about it. I'll build satellite schools wherever mayors and governors will let me in. The Little First Lady went to one of these satellites. She welcomed the mean streets. And I intend to have many more Merliners like Marianna once I'm in the White House."

Isaac's numbers leapt over the moon. Republicans adored him as much as the Democrats did. He had seventy-nine dollars in the bank. The Big Guy wouldn't need a blind trust. There was nothing to relinquish, nothing to hide. The country saw the dark blood beat over his temples and loved his brooding, his gravitas. It was ready to give him anything, even the Bronx.

27

BRENDA BROWN WAS LIKE A miraculous juggler who had all the details in her head. Isaac didn't have to meet with a living soul. She knew that he wanted Bull Latham as his VP.

"You won't announce until after the inauguration," she said.

"Why not?" he growled. "Brenda, don't mix in."

"Because we don't want to give him his moment of glory. We'll keep him in the background, like a common shill. He'll be naked without the FBI. We'll bury him and pick a new director."

And that's how his days went. Brenda was his quarterback and she tossed nothing but bullets. Isaac remained in seclusion at his mansion. He lived on a diet of butternut cookies. He'd shut down his offices at the Ansonia. He had little reason to go there now that AR's museum was gone. He brooded over his silver-hatted Inez and her children. But he'd promised not to interfere in her life. His cop's intuition told him to free Inez and shoot the shit out of Mr. David's men. But he kept to his promise.

And then Inez called. Somehow she had his private line at Gracie

Mansion. Isaac whimpered at the sound of her voice. He would have followed her to Mars.

"My big darling baby," she said. But she wasn't cooing. He could hear her tremble—he was listening very, very hard.

"Inez," he said with a thickened throat. "Can I see you?"

There was a pause, and then she told him, "Why not?"

"Just tell me where? We can go back to New Orleans if you want. I'll skip my own inauguration."

She laughed, but something was wrong.

"Darling, you know where I am."

"In Connecticut?" he asked like a bad little boy.

"Isaac, be careful. Someone very near is going to betray you. That's why I called."

"Did David tell you that?"

"I have my own little secrets," she said and hung up on Sidel. He couldn't even trace the call.

He kept brooding over possible betrayers. Could it be his son-in-law? Joe hadn't shopped drugs in a very long time. He'd gone into battle with the Big Guy, had taken an arrow in the chest. And Joey wasn't even interested in gelt. Was it the black Crusader? Isaac trusted Rondo Raines with his life. Rondo was the last holy man in the Bronx. Could it have been the Paramount lady, Brenda Brown? She ran from Hollywood, and she wouldn't have run into David Pearl's arms.

He began to pace up and down the stairs. Was it Marianna Storm? There was too much character in her butternut cookies. And what about Marilyn? Was his daughter getting even for Blue Eyes? She might have shunned Isaac, chastised him, but she wouldn't have harmed her own blood. And then the answer came with his cop's intuition. Inez was talking about herself. She was the betrayer, and she was warning the Big Guy. He groaned, because he knew that he would never see her again.

■ ■ ■

ISAAC SULKED. HE WASN'T RESOLUTE like Richard, blessed with a magical hump on his back. He was Hamlet's second cousin, a murderer who waited much too long. After another day of sulking, he went to his guns; he only had two—Joe Barbarossa and Rondo. He would mount a raid on Connecticut, rescue whatever was left of Inez. He didn't trust the Secret Service, not while Calder was still Prez. And he didn't trust Bull Latham's boys at the Bureau. He had to steal a whole squad of detectives from Manhattan North. It was his very own kind of vandalism. But he would be commander in chief in a couple of days. And who would have dared argue with an uncrowned king?

And just as he was about to ride up to Waterbury in his own wagon train, the Bull arrived out of nowhere. All his swagger was gone. He didn't have that look of a linebacker. He was as sad as Isaac Sidel.

"You found her, didn't you?" Isaac muttered.

"Outside Waterbury, at the edge of the road. A car had swiped her. . . . She wasn't even wearing any shoes."

"She must have been trying to escape from the wizard. Did she suffer a lot?"

The Bull was shivering now. "Mr. President, how the fuck would I know?"

"Can I see her?"

"I wouldn't. It's not a pretty sight."

"Can I see her?"

"Jesus Christ, they marked her all up," the Bull said in a cracked voice. "And they left her there in the cold."

"Her children," Isaac said. "We have to save her children."

"We sent them to her mother, in New Orleans."

"I could adopt them," Isaac said, like some cavalier.

"Absolutely," the Bull said. "Just like you adopted Inez."

And he fell upon Isaac, grabbed him around the ears. Isaac's Secret Service men were appalled. No one had ever wrestled with the director of the FBI. They rolled along the carpets of Gracie Mansion, knocked down tables and lamps. It was Isaac's chief of staff who kept a clear head.

"They're bonding," Brenda whispered to his aides. "The Prez and his VP."

Isaac's Glock fell out of his pants. It was the Bull who reached for it first. The Secret Service men mumbled into their button mikes. "The Citizen is down, the Citizen is down . . . possible casualty."

They stood frozen, without the least panache, as Bull Latham shoved the weapon back into Isaac's pants. "Mr. President, come with me."

They walked out of Gracie Mansion, a couple of sad sacks in ruffled coats.

A black van suddenly appeared in the driveway; Isaac figured it was one of the Bureau's sound trucks. Bull Latham opened the rear door.

"Hop in."

But the Big Guy seemed hesitant, and Latham shook his head. "You have my word, Mr. President. It won't bite. It's a temporary morgue. Come on, before the coroner gets here."

Isaac climbed into the van. His knees fell out from under him, and he swayed against the walls of the van. *Fucking FBI.* It was a morgue. His own dead darling was on a metal table, bundled in a white sheet. Some mother had already undressed her. But Isaac didn't undo the bundle. He wasn't a voyeur. There were bruises on her face, dried blood and bits of dirt under her eyes, so that the blood was like some beguiling mask in the dark of the truck. Her silver hair was all messed up. He'd never realized how small her hands were. Inez had the hands of a little girl.

He held her in his arms, wept like a wild man, while he fondled the dirt on her face. No one interrupted his grieving. No one knocked on the door of the van. He sat in there for six hours.

"Ah," he cried. "I should have taken care of you. Would AR have abandoned his Inez like that? Not in a million years."

28

THEY FOUND HIM. HE'D BEEN wandering in the woods with blood and filth on his face—Inez's errant "husband," Arno, the gunman without a gun. He'd been muttering to himself, and the agents who captured him had recorded what he said. *Tell the fuckin' Big Guy it wasn't my fault.* The Bull had him sequestered inside the Metropolitan Correctional Center, a holding pen for federal prisoners, male and female, in Lower Manhattan; it was a behemoth where the Bull could hide some bad guy who had never been charged. What the hell did they have on this demented wolf from Texas?

Had he murdered Trudy Winckleman? Only this stinking wolf knew. And the wolf wouldn't say a word.

David couldn't rescue him, because David didn't know where the hell he was. And the Bull was keeping the gunman as a gift for Isaac Sidel. The Bull had to show what he was worth, or Isaac would cast him aside and pick another VP. So he hid Arno, a.k.a the Waco Kid, in the FBI's own legal room and library deep in the bowels of the MCC—this library had a steel door three inches thick and didn't even possess a table, a book, or a chair.

Isaac rejoiced when the Bull told him that Arno had been apprehended. No one would interfere. The gunman was one more "ghost" in the Bull's personal files. Isaac could do whatever he wanted. But Arno's personal plea bothered him. *Tell the fuckin' Big Guy it wasn't my fault.*

He went into the bowels of the MCC. Clerks and correction officers stared at him. They were in awe of a policeman-president. There had never been anyone quite like Sidel. He wasn't unfriendly or wanton with them. He was just obsessed. It took three clerks to unlock the library door. Arno sat in the dark like the wolf he was. The Big Guy could barely see his face.

"Jesus," Isaac said, "will you get him some water? And give me some fucking light!"

He could have been the voice of God. The fluorescent lamp in the ceiling suddenly began to sizzle—and Arno's face was lit up like an enormous macaroon. The Bull must have pummeled Arno himself. Both his cheeks were swollen, and his eyes had vanished between several lumps of skin. A clerk came into the library with two gigantic jugs of water. Isaac handed Arno one of the jugs. They could have been drinking moonshine together.

"Well," Isaac growled, "I'm here. What did you want to discuss?"

Arno still sat scrunched in the corner, shielding himself with his own arms. He began to sob, and the sound of it was terrifying. He could have been a wounded animal.

"Don't kill me," Arno said, his shoulders heaving up and down.

"Jesus, would I glock you in the Bureau's own recreational center? Tell me what happened with Inez."

"Ef I tell ya, swear it won't be the end of Waco."

"What happened to Inez?"

It was hard to comprehend this crazy man, but Isaac had to crack into him like a codebook. Inez kept talking about her *chilrun*, he said, *chilrun* Isaac had never met. And she talked about the Big Guy. She was worried about him, worried that he wouldn't survive David's tricks. That was part of the conundrum. David wanted him alive and didn't want him alive. His gunmen were very confused. Would they get a reward for waxing Isaac, or a hole in the head? And their confusion leapt like wildfire to Inez. Was she a princess or their personal kitchen maid? But they sensed her weakness—the *chilrun*.

"Mr. Isaac, I swear on the Lawd's name, I only kissed her once."

Isaac was ready to pummel him now, but he didn't. He gulped that water in the whiskey jug.

It seems Arno had found a way to smuggle in the *chilrun*, but he wanted more than kisses.

"She had to show her titties and her blackberry bush. That ain't askin' much."

Isaac lost his control for a second and crowned him with the jug. And Arno couldn't stop crying. She tried to fool them, he said. Inez pretended to drink their whiskey, and when they caught her pretending, they kicked her and dragged her around the room. But they couldn't do much damage. They were as cockeyed as Irish fiddlers at a fiddlers' ball. And Inez ran out onto the road.

"But where to hell was she goin', Mr. Isaac? Her chilrun were in Mr. David's pocket somewheres, hundreds of miles from Waterbury. Was she tryin' to whistle her way to you? It was dark and lonely on a lonely road. We didn't run her down. We was too sick to drive."

Arno drifted in his own silent world, but Isaac wouldn't let him fall into a mindless funk.

"Tell me about the girl, *her* little girl."

"Darl?" the gunman said. "I only saw her once or twice. She had the cutest look. And if you shut your eyes, Mr. Isaac, you'd swear it was her mother, the Princess Inez. But the princess, she slapped us ef we started to stare."

Isaac walked out of the library and left Arno in the bowels of the MCC. He wouldn't have wept if the gunman remained invisible for the rest of his life. He'd have to grieve for Inez without the Waco Kid.

Isaac imagined her out on the road, in that Waterbury midnight, half-crazed, worrying that she might never see her kids again. He had witnessed the bruises on her face. The gunmen must have battered her during their own drunken stupor. The real assassin was David Pearl, not the car that broke her bones. . . .

The Big Guy couldn't have his seven days of mourning, or he would have missed his own coronation. Isaac was in no mood to become a king. And he had much more important business than a ride down Pennsylvania Avenue at the front of a parade. There wasn't much evidence against the wizard; no one couldn't tie him to Inez's death. He'd always given his orders from afar, like some Fu Manchu.

Isaac would have gone to David's roost all alone, or with his pair of Crusaders, Barbarossa and Rondo Raines. But Bull Latham had to protect Sidel. Besides, he didn't want to miss all the fun. So he decided to "flake" the wizard; he manufactured a couple of charges, called David a public menace who wanted to murder the president-elect, which wasn't so untrue, and he had a federal judge in Lower Manhattan issue a warrant. Who would have dared question the director of the Bureau?

It was all done in secret, but with the Bull's usual flair. Didn't he have jurisdiction over each nook and cranny in the United States? He could have deputized Sidel, made him some sort of federal marshal, but it would have been beneath Isaac's dignity. And he wouldn't supersede a mayor in his own town. So Isaac appeared as himself, a future president and king who was assisting in the arrest of a notoriously elusive king of crime.

It wasn't much of a task force: Isaac, Rondo, Joey, and the Bull, with a few of his agents and a battering ram. But Isaac didn't want a ruckus at the Ansonia. He wouldn't hurt a landmark that was listed in the National Registry. And he loved every stone.

He saluted the concierge, who asked him and the Bull for their autographs.

"Later," Isaac said. "Can't you see? We're busy. You'll stop the show."

They wouldn't take the elevator. They couldn't be sure how much firepower would greet them once the elevator opened on the seventeenth floor. So they climbed the Ansonia's magnificent stairs like a bunch of crusaders. But Isaac was riven by his own memories. He marveled at the enormous windows on the landings midway between every floor, as the light blazed down upon them. They were all dizzy by the time they reached the tenth floor. The Bull began to cough into his fist.

"Mr. President, we'll be lame if we have to climb another seven flights."

"Move your butt," Isaac rasped. "I don't want any surprises at the top of the stairs."

And so they plodded on with their battering ram and arrived on the seventeenth floor, after coughing their brains out. The echo of their own sound and fury should have alerted David's gunsels, but there were no gunsels on the landing. They didn't even have to use the battering ram. David's door was open. All his gunsels had abandoned him; they must have heard about the phony warrant and decided to save their own skin; the wizard's wealth of cash couldn't have kept them out of jail, not with Isaac and the FBI.

They knew how vindictive Bull Latham could be; the Bull was a bigger ball-breaker than Sidel.

David sat under the low ceilings in his slippers and tattered sweater. His apartment looked like an endless dollhouse. He wouldn't even acknowledge Bull.

"Kiddo," he said to Sidel. "I knew you would come for me. I'm sorry about your loss. I was fond of that bitch."

"Shut up," Isaac said, "before I bite your fucking head off."

"Isaac, Isaac," David said, wagging his own head of white hair. "How long do you think you can hold me? I'll have a whole battery of lawyers at the MCC before we get there."

The wizard was much too notorious to be stashed away in an underground dungeon with that gunsel of his, the Waco Kid. David Pearl had too many "gonnegtions." But he should have realized that Bull Latham was also a wizard.

"Sweetheart, we're not going to the MCC."

The wizard's face froze with panic. "I can't sit in the dark. I'll die. . . . Isaac, I've bribed Bull Latham. I've given him pocket money."

"So what?" Isaac said. "Nobody's perfect. All that matters is where you are right now."

■ ■ ■

ISAAC NEVER EVEN ASKED THE Bull about their destination. Their little wagon train rode right into the Bronx. At first, Isaac thought they were going to bury David somewhere in the dunes. Under Robert Moses' highway. That would have been a just reward. The wizard could have had the whole Reservation for himself, all the bitter ground, with every mote of dust from the buildings he had ruined. But their wagon train went right over the badlands and bumped onto Fort Schuyler Road. They'd come to the edge of the world, according to the Bronx. It was land's end, with its own lighthouse and little fort at Throgs Point, which jutted into Long Island Sound.

Isaac loved the fury of the sea. He would have swum to China, if he hadn't been preoccupied with the wizard. He had to sing his mourner's song out on the road. The lighthouse was under repair, and its roving yellow eye had been plucked right out of its skull. It stood like some Samson Agonistes in the mist. The fort had been built after the War of 1812, in the hope of expelling the British or any other invader. Its guns would forever protect the Bronx from any naval attack. It held five hundred Confederate prisoners during the Civil War and deserters from the Union army. It became defunct as a fort around 1910 and was soon converted into a maritime college. But the old fort was also in disrepair; many of its stones had fallen into the sea; its gun turrets were like ragged, useless sockets; its roofs leaked. It was under six feet of water half the year. The maritime college had moved momentarily across the creek to Locust Point. And the fort was turned into a secret brig.

Isaac didn't like the whole fucking setup. It smelled of fascism, of military maneuvers in his own town. Someone should have told him that this old fort had a new landlord—Bull Latham's Bureau. But he didn't argue. The wind blew against Isaac's beleaguered bones as he stepped out of Latham's van with the wizard. David Pearl was shivering in his tattered clothes; one of his slippers had come off. The wizard had no socks. Isaac saw a naked foot, as bleached and dry as an old skeleton. He had to prosecute such a pathetic case. But then he recalled Inez's body in the Bull's makeshift morgue.

They entered this abandoned fort, which had its own skeleton crew; agents on the verge of retirement, Isaac figured.

"Jesus, Bull, we haven't even booked the old guy."

"There's plenty of time for that. We'll bounce him from place to place. When I'm finished with Pearl, he'll be public enemy number one."

"Just like the old days," Isaac said, "with J. Edgar Hoover."

They went under a crumbling arch and right through the main gate; Isaac could hear the water rip. He could imagine Confederate prisoners with chains on their legs in this cruel courtyard. They traveled down a flight of crooked steps, with Isaac holding David by his pants. The Big Guy's blood was freezing. That's how cold it was. They locked the wizard in a narrow cell without windows, gave him a couple of blankets and a dirty pillowcase.

"Let him cool off for a couple of days," the Bull said.

Isaac didn't even have the heart to say good-bye. He returned to Bull's wagon train, sat between Joey and Rondo in the back of the van. All he could think about were the Crusaders in Nam. The Crusaders had been as willful as the Vietcong. That's why they were such successful scalp hunters. They were the only ones who could fight Charlie on his own turf. The Crusaders didn't give a fuck about winning over hearts and minds. They had no heart. They were methodical, merciless plunderers. They treated the Vietcong like one more bag of tricks.

But no faraway tale could soothe the Big Guy. When their wagon train arrived in the badlands, and Isaac saw ruin after ruin, he could no longer block out the old man.

Public enemy number one, with a missing sock.

"Bull," he shouted, "we have to turn around. I can't leave David in that lousy dungeon. He'll die of double pneumonia."

29

THE BULL WOULDN'T ARGUE WITH his own commander in chief. He hadn't been reckless. He was only marking time. The moment Isaac was inaugurated, the Bull intended to pluck a signed order out of him that would have landed David behind the moon and kept him there, permanently out of sight. But Isaac was *another* bull—a Taurus, and a Taurus couldn't be swayed. The Bull would have to factor in President Sidel's stubbornness from now on. He'd shut his secret prison before Isaac had the chance to intervene. He didn't care who the next director was. Bull Latham meant to run the Bureau from his new digs at the Naval Observatory. And so he shuttled Isaac and David Pearl back to the Ansonia.

Isaac rode the elevator up to the seventeenth floor with David in his arms. It was like clutching some prehistoric bird, or a rumpled dinosaur egg. He could hear David's heart beat. He sat him down in a chair under that impossible ceiling, where Isaac had to keep ducking his head. He wrapped David's toes in a heated towel.

"Kiddo, this ain't gonna buy you credit with me."

"Who cares for your credit?"

"Don't you think I miss her, too? She was my Abishag. I would come down to the thirteenth floor in the middle of the night and lie next to her for half an hour. No hanky-panky."

"Shut up," Isaac said. "You shouldn't have had her killed."

"She was the only weapon I had against you. I was losing blood by the minute. The dams kept breaking in the Bronx—all on account of you."

"I hope you lose a hundred million," Isaac said.

"Chicken feed. Didn't I swear months ago that I was betting on you to be the next president? And by staging all those assassination attempts, I was only upping the ante. Yeah, sometimes I did want you killed. But who else remembers AR and Inez? I had that museum built for you."

"No more stories," Isaac said. But he was still addicted. His voice was getting shaky. He kept dreaming of Lindy's oblong look. His own table at Ratner's wasn't much of a shrine. He would have given the fingers of one hand to have sat with David at Arnold's table for half an hour.

"Jesus, tell me what happened when Inez walked into that delicatessen?"

The wizard was in his element again. He could curl up in his chair—tell his tale.

"Even the mice were mesmerized," David said. "No one could resist that blond storm. Every miserable eye was on Inez, except for Arnold. He was the last to look up. The Brain was always in his own deep thoughts. But he could feel the rush, that explosion of air, as Inez danced into the delicatessen with her long legs. I watched his brow furrow for an instant. He knew the mayhem that Inez could bring. But she also brought AR her own delight. And that thinker at the table would come out of his dark mood and smile. Arnold never smiled like that for me. . . ."

Isaac knew that Arnold's table would haunt him into eternity. The White House was also a museum. But presidents couldn't trouble Isaac, not the way Rothstein could. He'd have to convince his chief of staff to let the Little First Lady live with him. He couldn't weave any fabric into his life without Marianna Storm. Let them shout *Lolita*. He wouldn't give up Marianna or his Glock.

"Her brats," David said, "I adopted them. Both were born out of wedlock. They'd hardly had a real father."

"What are you talking about?"

"Winckleman's kids. They're legally mine. That's how Bull punishes me. He hides them."

"They're in New Orleans with Trudy's mom. Bull told me himself."

"She never had a mom," David said. "She grew up in an orphanage. One of her own nurses had silver hair . . . ah, I'm being polite. It was a bordello near Basin Street. She survived on beignets from the French Market in the Vieux Carré. . . . The kids aren't in New Orleans. Bull wants them near him, so he can eat my heart out. They're at a row house beside the Ohio Canal, in Georgetown. They have nurses around the clock."

"And I suppose you'd like them back, you miserable prick."

"No, the kids are better off where they are. . . . Soon they'll have an uncle in the White House."

"Shut up."

■ ■ ■

IT DIDN'T MATTER WHAT HIS chief of staff said. She could supervise all the public business of a president, ponder over his cabinet as if she were playing pickup sticks, talk to his policy advisers about East Berlin, tell Isaac whom to shun, but she couldn't prevent him from going to DC with Marianna a day before his coronation. They rode in a limousine with Rondo Raines. He didn't have any of the president's markings on the limo, and he wouldn't have wanted any.

"Jesus," Isaac said to Marianna. "What should I tell them? That I loved their mama, and I'm one of the reasons she got killed?"

"Uncle Isaac, do you *always* have to complicate things?"

"But I'm a perfect stranger. What if they don't like me?"

"That's the chance you'll have to take."

He wanted to wear his schnozzola, but she said it was undignified, and might scare the kids. He'd have to risk his own skin, come to them as Isaac Sidel. . . .

They parked on Olive Street. Marianna got out of the car. She was wearing a plain winter coat. Children and adults began to collect around her. "The Little First Lady!" Isaac wasn't chagrined. He'd much rather have melted into the background. How had she gathered so much poise with two dysfunctional parents—a murderous mom and dad!

But perhaps she was drawn to murderous men, or she wouldn't have baked butternut cookies for Isaac and lived at Gracie Mansion as mistress of the house. And Isaac was much more homicidal than Michael or Clarice would ever be. But he wasn't twisted by their cruelty and greed. He had a very different kind of barometer. He'd never put out someone's lights just to gain a little loot.

It was Marianna who ended this autograph party with her fans. "Goodness," she said. "We have so much to do." She took Isaac by the hand and led him down the hill to the C & O Canal. This must have been the point of the rendezvous. Marianna had arranged it. They were near a sluice, and the sound of running water calmed Sidel.

The two children arrived with their nurse. Isaac's knees buckled. Both of them had Inez's big eyes and her marvelous frown. The boy was nine or ten. His name was Daniel. The girl was Marianna's age, and had she ever worn a silver helmet, she would have been Inez. She brooded and smiled, and her mouth was puckered, like her mother's. Her name was Darl.

Isaac had a terrible case of vertigo on the C & O Canal. He thought he would spill into the water and drown, even if it wasn't possible to drown in the C & O. Marianna had to prop him up. She pinched his arm and spat into his ear, "Uncle Isaac, you're embarrassing us. What will Daniel and Darl think of the next White House?"

But he couldn't stop crying. It was like standing with little replicas of Inez. He could feel her presence in these children. He'd been thrust into the middle of a ghost story and he'd never recover from it. He wanted to run howling from Georgetown and hide in some lost dune. It was Darl who understood his agony, Darl who was so quick.

"You knew my mother, didn't you, Mr. President?"

"Please," he said, glued to the melody of her voice. "Call me Isaac."

He stared at the little houses on the canal, wanted to live there with these children and Marianna. Let his chief of staff occupy the Oval Office. Isaac would stay on this side of Rock Creek.

"I loved your mother," he said. "She was dear to me. But I didn't know how to keep her. I was selfish and arrogant."

"That's how most men are," she said with a little pout.

She took Isaac's hand. Daniel joined them. Isaac noticed for the first time that Daniel was clutching a stuffed bear; both its button eyes were missing; it had bald patches on its pelt of hair. It was the casualty of some war.

"What's the bear's name?" he asked.

"Isaac," Darl said before her baby brother could open his mouth.

Isaac smiled like a madman and did his own tiny jig on the canal.

The four of them were holding hands. Marianna stood near Daniel. She was almost as tall as Sidel, and could have been the benevolent mama of her own little brood. Or perhaps a big sister, since she knew that Darl would soon become her own blood and her best friend in DC.

It could have been a family picnic on the canal. There wasn't a Secret Service man in sight. Only Rondo Raines, with hammered silver down the sides of his boots. He was smoking a Bugler, and he didn't look much like a bodyguard. He could have been a pathfinder on the C & O. And Isaac could have been the papa bear.

The January sun beat down upon his pate. He bit into the wind that swept off the canal. He could finish up his seven days of mourning right now. He clung to Daniel and Darl, clung to Marianna, and he knew what would please him most in the president's palace—the waft of butternut cookies from the White House kitchen, with both of Inez's babies beside him.

EBOOKS BY
JEROME CHARYN

FROM MYSTERIOUSPRESS.COM
AND OPEN ROAD MEDIA

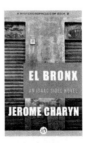
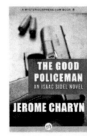

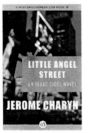
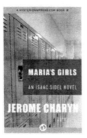

These and more available wherever ebooks are sold

MYSTERIOUSPRESS.COM

OPEN ROAD
INTEGRATED MEDIA

MYSTERIOUSPRESS.COM

Otto Penzler, owner of the Mysterious Bookshop in Manhattan, founded the Mysterious Press in 1975. Penzler quickly became known for his outstanding selection of mystery, crime, and suspense books, both from his imprint and in his store. The imprint was devoted to printing the best books in these genres, using fine paper and top dust-jacket artists, as well as offering many limited, signed editions.

Now the Mysterious Press has gone digital, publishing ebooks through **MysteriousPress.com**.

MysteriousPress.com offers readers essential noir and suspense fiction, hard-boiled crime novels, and the latest thrillers from both debut authors and mystery masters. Discover classics and new voices, all from one legendary source.

FIND OUT MORE AT

WWW.MYSTERIOUSPRESS.COM

FOLLOW US:

@emysteries and Facebook.com/MysteriousPressCom

MysteriousPress.com is one of a select group of publishing partners of Open Road Integrated Media, Inc.

INTEGRATED MEDIA

Open Road Integrated Media is a digital publisher and multimedia content company. Open Road creates connections between authors and their audiences by marketing its ebooks through a new proprietary online platform, which uses premium video content and social media.

Videos, Archival Documents, and New Releases

Sign up for the Open Road Media newsletter and get news delivered straight to your inbox.

Sign up now at
www.openroadmedia.com/newsletters

.

CPSIA information can be obtained at www.ICGtesting.com
Printed in the USA
BVOW072037141012

302961BV00004B/2/P